Ninety Days

Douglas Arnold

Published by YouWriteOn.com

Sponsored by The Arts Council of England

First Edition

A CIP copy of this book is available at The British Library

For Theresa, Zoë, Robert and Christopher

Chapter One

For his sins Geoff had succumbed to the temptation of a third portion of his wife's fresh cream chocolate sponge cake. It was the seduction of the fresh strawberries, which had been mine swept from the reduced bin in the local supermarket, and arranged sliced on the top of the cake that did it. Then again the fifth column collaboration of the bed of fresh whipped cream didn't help. He had been awake with indigestion for most of the night. It was pretty much an ordinary sort of day for finding something useful to do for a change. Life as the saying goes is hard, and over the last couple of years, living had become even harder.

Gone were the heady days of the eighties, with work queuing up to find people to do it. The opposite was the case, with people queuing up to sign the unemployment register. From a very reasonable income indeed, with the usual credibility and self worth, the world of work had collapsed almost overnight. The firm, his family home, and most of all his self respect, went with a bankruptcy court hearing and an insolvency number from the office of the official receiver. Life these days consisted of a ceaseless rut of uselessness. The most arduous tasks of the day, since having so little to do had become; get up, wash, shave, and if he could lift himself to the heights of achievement, make and eat some breakfast. On the whole so far, things had been rather boring, if not actually depressing. It was a typical night that follows such over indulgence. His eyes would not stay closed, in a wilfully contrary clash to his body's need to sleep. He had risen at 4 a.m., for a cigarette and a large mug of tea. His eyes were like dinner plates. His head would not stop thinking of five things at once, and managed to wonder if he had been dragged through a hedge with a bar of soap in his mouth. The only rational solution seemed to be to give up, get up, and try to wake up in an almost tolerant temper.

True friend as she was, Sally his Jack Russell bitch, was lying patiently awaiting his move towards his raincoat, to be taken for her morning walk. It was very early, but she thought he would chance her luck, by cocking one ear, and looking as expectant as possible. It worked. Geoff decided to give the old girl a treat. A short drive from the flat is the pebble beach at Devil's Point, within Plymouth Sound. Devil's Point, regardless of its demonic name, has been a place of peace and serenity for the people of Plymouth for years. The large green sward and the beach are very much like a mini Plymouth Hoe, minus the tourists. Access, like most locally used places anywhere, is off the beaten track. The approach is via the bustle of the world famous night club strip of Union Street, with its glitz and strip joints. A back street turn, bordering the red light district, brings the visitor to the end of the road. Except for a little lane off to the south of the square, almost tucked into the corner, in the hope that no-one will notice it. One would be forgiven for feeling that it was just another back street. The landscape is a mixture of dockland industrial units, and bed sits. The area belies the revelations at the end of the lane. Bordered by a sandstone cliff on one side, and two ninety degree turns in the narrow lane, skirting the convent on the other, the view opens to reveal the vast natural harbour of Plymouth Sound. The historic Artillery Tower has steps which lead down to the beach below. The vast walls, forts, and the breakwater, hewn in Dartmoor granite, all long standing monuments to the labours of French Napoleonic prisoners of war, whose forced labour built them all.

All around this massive natural harbour and oceanic amphitheatre are the forts and pill boxes of defenders of the realm through history. From this famous place, world beating expeditions have departed: From Drake's dispatch of the Spanish, through to Chichester's lone compass of the globe. The pilgrim's departed, and Napoleon himself was imprisoned on a hulk in the waters of Plymouth Sound. The majesty of this historic and beautiful port is as much a feeling as a sight.

Standing on the rocks of the foreshore today, the might of The Royal Navy can be seen sailing by every day. The view opens out, so that beyond the cliffs of Cornwall, where Ravens nest on the crags of Mount Edgecumbe, the winking lonely light on the Eddystone reef can be seen, miles out to sea, at once the harbinger of doom, and yet the herald to the homeward bound, and the promise of the shore. The tamed sea laps gently against the paddling pool, which the city built for the benefit of one and all. Every tide washes the pool clean, and sometimes trapped sand eels are chased with enthusiasm and futility, by children with small nets.

The pebble beach lay, as a naked seaside, with kelp and weed exposed, and the sea trapped in the pool. Planks of wood, small pieces of rope, and flotsam and jetsam of passing water traffic, are strewn on the strand. The greyness of the day was beginning to show signs of winning over the dark. It was that time, when neither shade nor light, or distance, or hue, were winning the contest of the dawn. Daytime was but a promise. In the changing dimness, part of the sea seemed a little too dark for what it was. There was no form or shape to what appeared to be there, but for a mere hint that part of the sea was filled with that which is somehow out of place. Geoff walked around the wall of the pool, trying to reflect some light from perhaps the dockyard or a street light up on the road, off the water and into his eye. There it was, no there was more than one. Distinct forms of....

For a moment he thought they were bodies, washed up in the night from a sea accident, but then there would have been searchers for sure. The lifeboat and police launches would be looking for them at least. Then it seemed as though they were just discarded clothes. Perhaps a no longer waterproof jacket from a careless sailor, tossed overboard without a care for the world in which we live. Then anger welled up inside him. It was rubbish, half a dozen black plastic bin liners at least, tied up and chucked overboard by some lazy careless deckhand: Some crew, who was too lazy to dispose of the ship's rubbish properly. No wonder the sea is so filthy that you can't swim in it anymore. The English Channel is no more than a liquid dustbin these days, curse the irresponsible and their arrogance. He decided to grab one, which was just reachable, with a washed up piece of driftwood, and hook it ashore. If he could land them and stack them up at the top of the steps, the refuse collectors would pick them up, and dispose of the waste properly. The problem was not that the rubbish was in bin liners, but that it was very symmetrical, and too well wrapped. No-one wrapped and taped up rubbish that carefully. The half inch green tape bound the plastic wrap into a neat package.

Geoffrey decided to open one up at a corner, to have a look, and to confirm his new fear, that these were parcels of drugs, washed ashore from smugglers. The import of goods into these islands has been carrying on for 3000 years. Iron Age metal workers, traded with seafarers from the main continent. The Phoenicians traded for Cornish tin, to alloy with copper, making their bronze ware and weapons. St.Budoc imported Christianity into the region, and wreckers imported their ill gotten gains from the rocks of the treacherous coast. The barrels of rum stamped George Rex Old Grenadian, or G.R.O.G., surely didn't all enter via the dutiful channels of the customs house. For centuries the coast has been, and probably still is, a smuggler's paradise. The tiny coves and beaches, connected by inland coastal lanes, are a maze in themselves. Even those who know their way can get lost on a dark and moonless night. It is unknown, and probably impossible to assess, the amount of illicit booze, cigarettes, tobacco, perfume, and jewellery, which comes in over the border without having its duty paid. In the latter part of this century, there has been a far more sinister trade. Arguably worse than the murderous and heartless trade in humanity that was the slave trade. The sick barter in human misery, of drugs trafficking, has taken over. The profits of the dealers are immense. The returns make the risks worth taking, and the results denied and lied about, rather than faced. The package was heavy, very heavy, like a sack of potatoes. If this hit the streets, there was enough cannabis here to feed the addicts of Plymouth for a very long time indeed. Geoffrey had always carried a penknife, and he took the two inch blade out of his pocket, opened it, and locked it with the locking sleeve. The corner of the package sliced open under pressure from the steel blade, which was always as sharp as a razor. He gingerly put his nose to the bag to smell the contents.

To his surprise there was no spicy, herby smell of cannabis resin, just a stale pungent stink. He was unsure of himself for a few moments. The smell was acrid and stale, but it was not the stink of dirty dustbins. That sharp tang was familiar on the nose, in a distinct but unrelated way. He had definitely smelled it before, but out of context he could not quite place it. The memory of the scent was locked in his mind, but he could not quite recall from where he had smelled that smell before. There was one thing he was sure of, it was not drugs. Cutting a little further into the packaging, and exposing the corner of the contents, it became evident that the bag he was looking at contained paper. He thought it was probably from a computer printer. With all the floating gin palaces that come and go in The Sound, this could easily be the discarded junk from a yuppie sailor, living in some kind of wasteful world of decadent disposability. Opening up a little more of the plastic, the quality of the thin paper revealed the rolls and scrolls of printer's ink. The flamboyant calligraphy, and crisp feel was instantly recognisable, and only ever found on money.

Carefully wrapped to the point of being waterproof, these modern day Moses baskets, had an air of being lost rather than dumped. There was a sudden recollection of where that smell had been in his memory. His father had owned a shop when he had been a boy, and the memory was the odour of the till. That was it: The unmistakable odour of money, but much stronger. The stink of thousands of used notes. It didn't take an Einstein to work out that five bags, in the end there were five in total, full of money that weigh the same as a sack of potatoes each, comes to more than the price of a round of drinks. He thought there must be hundreds of thousands there, if not millions. On the principal that if he had lost say a fifty pound note, he would probably be searching, with a fine toothed comb, until he found it. Then if someone had lost several large bags of money, they would be out mob handed, with a large pick axe handle, or worse. At the same moment that he came to that conclusion, a very cold sinking feeling accompanied the tickle of hairs, as they rose on the back of his neck. His mouth suddenly felt dry, and his hands clammy. There was an overbearing conviction that hidden eyes were watching from the shadows. In the half light of the dawn, there were suddenly shadows behind every rock, and movement behind every bush. It came upon him in a mad rush, that this was a very open space indeed, and he was amazed that no-one else had come out to see the new day, not even a milkman, on his rounds. He was convinced that he was about to be pounced upon by a gang of desperate rough necks, baying for blood.

A loud wailing scream made him freeze in his tracks. His heart jumped in his chest, as he instinctively drew in a sharp breath of the cold morning air. Above him a lone seagull, resentful of the man's intrusion to the morning patrol of his patch of beach, had voiced his protest. The bird had no idea of just how effective was the alarm call at causing alarm. A little involuntary, nervous smile crept over his suddenly chill lips.

There is a public telephone box at the top of the car park, and he decided to 'phone the police, and get these parcels dealt with. The quicker the authorities dealt with them, and with the least fuss, the better. It occurred to him that it would be foolish to leave the packages where they were, as someone may well come along and lay claim to them in his absence. Carrying each a few yards at a time, and then returning for the next, he worked his way up the beach. Back and forth he struggled until they were eventually at the base of the winding sea wall steps. Sweat from the effort began to run down his face, and he began to regret giving up squash, in favour of cigarettes and coffee. Even then he was not convinced that these rivulets were entirely due to the first hard work that he had done in months. Trying to move all these shady looking bags, at 5.30 in the morning, without attracting attention, was proving embarrassing. He was still convinced that he was being watched. He felt a little like a fox in a henhouse, trying to look innocent. He was convinced that he looked about as discreet as a pine tree on a prairie. At last they were at the top of the sea wall, and he sat them around the waste bins of the restaurant that was resident in the tower, in a vain attempt at disguise. None the less they were in sight of the telephone, so that he could see them at all times. He didn't manage to think about quite what he would do if someone did turn up to collect.

It is amazing that honesty can be so readily soluble in cash. It only took about thirty seconds to walk across the small tarmac car park, to the 'phone box on the corner of the lane, and in that short space of time, many thoughts went through Geoffrey Wilson's head. If there were a direct relationship between sainthood on one side, and the amount involved on the other, then his mind's thoughts went off the graph. Granny's purse, with a pension book, bus pass, and a five pound note, can be handed in with shovelsful of self-righteousness and pride. Several lost sacks full of money, as in this case, can work on the greed button so fast, that the mind slips into an overdrive of scheming in no time flat. It wasn't as if this were anything ordinary. This was after all, an awful lot of money. His mind began to justify what he knew he was going to do. He had not quite resolved the argument in his head yet. The lost cash had come from what was in all probability, a none too legitimate source. At least he didn't think any of the financial institutions transported money like this. So what if he just kept it? The next question which arose was how he would deal with such an amount? And anyway, how much was there? He imagined the questions if he walked into the local branch of his bank with a cheery smile. 'Oh good morning, I would like to open an account please. Would five bin liners stuffed with cash do as a deposit'? The police would be there in about two minutes. He needed time to think.

This was all too much.

He tried to calm himself down. If there was one thing he was certain of, it was that if he panicked he would make mistakes. He had to try to get a clearer perspective of what his situation was, and then to decide what to do next. He felt very much alone. This was his penalty kick, in the dying seconds of his personal cup final. Keeping his head to score would mean that he would be a winner. Miss it and he would be a loser, with his 'if only' story for the rest of his life. He looked over to the bags with their treasured secret and wondered what would happen if he did call the police. What if a bent copper turned up? Was he taking too much of a risk in trusting them? After all they were only human.

The turning point of his certainty happened when he looked over to his car. The dull creamy brown, set off with rust spots on his 100,000 mile non descript Lada. It was an M.O.T. failure at £70, which he had desperately struggled to find the money for. The whole family had made sacrifices of their needs, so that his heavily pregnant wife could have a little car. It gave her and the children a tiny bit of freedom at least. He was flat broke, unemployed, and his children were dressed in hand me downs. They had second hand toys, and second hand furniture. The rest of their possessions were from the re-cycled end of the market. Did he and his family not deserve a decent lifestyle? But what if he were caught?

There are a quarter of a million people living in the city, and as small as that is in terms of cities, it is big enough to slip away without being spotted, and to melt into the background. If he were to load the bags into the car, and quietly disappear, who would know? All he had to do was to keep his head down for a while. The questions kept ringing around his head in a whirlpool of indecision. What were the legal implications? What if he handed the money in? What if someone claimed it? What if they reported it missing? Who the hell loses that much money in the tide honestly? How much is there? What if they didn't hand it in and they found him? Where would he go? What would he do?

The dog and the bags had loaded themselves into the car somehow. In his daze of mental confusion he had carried out the actions that he knew he was going to, whilst still trying to justify them in his mind. Having decided to keep it, he now wanted to get home as quickly as possible. At the same time, breaking the speed limit would be a stupid thing to do. To be stopped now, with a very guilty look on his face, would be a disaster.

It was normal at this time, for Susan Birch to be awake. She worked in a department store in the city centre. It was her responsibility to display all the cakes and pastries of her tidy, ordered, and immaculate counter. She had become well known and respected by her colleagues and customers alike, loved her job and had a trained hawk eye for that which is out of place. Susan always rose early, and sat in the front window of her flat, overlooking The Sound. She usually drank an early morning coffee, and gathered her thoughts. She achieved a peace of mind that would enable her to handle the bustle of the day. She had a natural happiness which was what made her so well liked by everyone. She had spotted the unusual car on the car park, but taken no particular notice of it. When she saw several black packages being heaved up the steps, and hidden around the bins of the restaurant, she became very suspicious indeed. When the furtive and nervous looking character went to the telephone, and then quickly loaded the parcels and his little dog into the motor, she noted the number. When he had driven off, she thought for a couple of minutes, about whether to get involved or not. Her sense of public duty overtook her doubt, and after finishing her drink, rang the police with the car's details.

Sod's Law says it, and this short journey proved it. Just when you don't want a police car following you, one arrives, as if queued in by the director of nerve racking experiences. It's a bit like treating a work colleague to a coffee at lunchtime, who by accident of gender happens to be female. The one day that you decide to do that, you meet your wife in the restaurant, with her mother. This particular policeman was simply doing his beat. He took as little notice as possible, without being derelict in his duty. At this time of the day, the object was to return to the station, and to finish the shift on time. A policeman's lot these days, was a big enough mass of paperwork. With high crime rates, and so many regulations to follow, the last thing he wanted was to look for an even bigger work load. The beaten up Lada in front looked about as roadworthy as a soapbox on pram wheels. Experience had taught him though, that when they looked that bad, they were almost invariably Kosher. The owners wouldn't have the nerve to drive them on the road otherwise. He turned off right to the station, musing as he went, on the pros and cons of annual number plates. At least you would be able to tell from behind, if the vehicle was taxed and insured. He noted the number anyway, just in case.

Geoff knew that he was being tailed. The police car was just a yard too close to be travelling in the same direction by coincidence. In the rear view mirror, he could tell that he was being given the once over. He exhaled a long slow breath when the police car turned off. He had been so nervous that for a few seconds he had forgotten to breathe. Within a few minutes, he had reached home. Luckily he was able to park up right outside the flat, in the same spot that he had left earlier. He saw that there was nobody about in the street. The lime trees swayed their soothing dance, their very greenness giving a shade of quiet. He opened the car door and let the dog out. Sally ran gratefully back to the flat. She was cold and still wet from her run on the sea front. For a dog, sally was not the outdoor type. She liked to curl up in front of the fire as much as anything. If it was raining, she went out for a walk with dulled enthusiasm.

The parcels were quickly unloaded and carried up the stairs, to the kitchen of his first floor, two bed roomed council flat. The table was a second hand oak affair, with worn veneer, and thick ugly legs. Still it was solid, and the two leaves pulled out to make it big enough for the job in hand, He took the bag that he had first examined, and began to open it properly. The green parcel tape was a pain. It was stuck very firmly to the bags, and he made a mental note of how good it was. Unlike that brown stuff that you can buy, this was good quality tape. In fact it was so well stuck, that he was forced to open the bag with his trusty penknife. Strange that ever since he had been a boy, he had carried a penknife. There was no specific purpose that he could put the habit down to. There was no specific reason, like peeling fruit, or sharpening pencils, but he felt naked without it. He used the little blade constantly, for all sorts of jobs. Never had there been such an important task for his little knife than this. Having often lost and replaced them, he decided to treasure this one as a keepsake.

Tipping the bag out onto the table, there were individual wraps of money, in hermetically sealed packages. Whoever had packed this cash, had intended for it to stay dry. The pack from the bottom was the one he had cut into on the beach, and he opened it fully to count it. There were fifties, twenties, and tens, all in Stirling. He raised a couple to the light, to see that they had their watermark, and the tell tale strip of metal, which told him that this was the real thing. This was not, as had just crossed his mind, a bag full of forgeries. This was the genuine article. He counted the bundle. Ten grand, in used ones. Here was an awful lot of dosh. Here was the proverbial, 'enough to spend'.

As is usual when something is going down in the home, the children did not want to be left out. They were beginning to stir from their innocent slumbers. The very last thing that he needed was for them to talking to their friends. It was vital to maintain absolute secrecy, for the moment at least. The subtleties of adult dishonesty were a mystery to them. He stuffed the money into another bin bag, and quickly put them into his bedroom. He wanted to leave his wife to lie in for a while, but decided that she should be woken up, to at least look after the rest of the family, whilst he dealt with this problem.

Holding the bag open, he picked up a packet, and threw it on the bed. It bounced off the top of the mound of quilt, and landed on the floor with the thump of a paperback. She groaned her protest at this rude awakening. Chuckling to himself, he bounced another one. She turned over and muttered a complaint in semi-awareness. The third bounced off the top of her head, and she vented her displeasure in a most unladylike way. He laughed and tossed another.

'What the hell do you think you're doing, you stupid fool? That's not funny you know. Leave me alone'.

He tossed another pack onto her lap. She picked it up with half opened eyes and threw it back. It bounced off the door with a loud bang. Her aim never was too good, especially first thing in the morning. He picked it up, and gently tossed it back.

'What the hell is this?'

'Why don't you open it and see?'

She rubbed her eyes, still mumbling about stupid games, and something about time and morning. There was a passing observation about growing up, which was thrown in for good measure. She ripped open the polythene, and her eyes nearly popped out of her head. At the same time, her chin had a falling out, from its marriage to her top lip. There were two firsts here. In ten years of marriage, Geoffrey Wilson had never seen his wife wake up so fast. He could not recall her ever being totally lost for words before. There was a long, dumbstruck silence, which lasted until her brain managed to put the obvious question together,

'What's this?'

Despite the obvious and self evident fact that it was a lot of money, she was also aware that it was a silly question. The plain fact was that she could not think of anything else to say.

'That my dear is a very small part of the rest of this bagful, along with the other four just like it. I know it's incredible, but I just walked Sally down at Devil's Point, and there they were, washed up on the beach'.

'Jesus', was all that she could say.

Recovering slightly she asked the most important question,

'How much is there?'

'I don't know, fancy counting it'?

The next half hour was dedicated to an impatient time; of dressing children, finding mislaid kit, lost shoes, and the bolting of breakfast, to avoid the much dreaded detention that would result if they were late for school. It may seem an impossibility to the uninitiated, but counting money, in the end, can be tiresome, and laborious. There has to be an awful lot of it to achieve that status, but £4,521,375 Stirling, definitely falls into that category. It also takes a very long time.

They counted and double checked, using a block of paper to mark a stroke for each thousand, then crossing out with the fifth, and working in two columns. They were on the fifth sheet when they reached the magic million. It was obvious that they were not a quarter of the way through, mainly because they hadn't finished the first bag yet. The fifth was just as full, but with more of the tens and fives, and less of the twenties and fifties. This explained the loose change of £21,375 in one of the bags. The other four had exactly four million between them. That is if you count £21,375 as change, and ignore the half a million in fifty pound notes in a separate bundle in the last bag. That concluded the contents. There were no accountancy slips, bank papers or account names, numbers or addresses. It was the most anonymous of fortunes ever to fall into the hands of any finder. Having finished counting and searching the contents of the bags, they now did the most English of things. All over the world, anyone else would have been bolting doors, and lifting floorboards, to secrete the hoard away. In this household, they had a cup of tea, lit a cigarette, and waited. It was as if they were awaiting instructions. From which source, they had no idea. Perhaps they were waiting for divine guidance. There were very few people in history, who had a direct telephone line with God, and none with material instructions, since perhaps Moses was told what to do with the stone tablets.

Sarah Wilson had filled the kettle, and set it on the gas hob. In a few minutes it announced that it was boiling with its doleful wail. It is a noise that serves its function, yet at the same time manages to annoy, and demand immediate attention. She ceremoniously poured a little water into the pot to warm it. She gently swayed the water around, to even the warming. Emptying the contents, the tea spooned into the pot, and freshly boiling water was poured over the tea. In a few minutes they were sipping the refreshing brew, pampering themselves with an extra spoon of sugar each.

They considered their position, and what they should do about it. Geoffrey repeated the options and the scenarios, with their possible consequences, as he saw them. It was obvious that if the owners of the money came after their property, then there was a possibility, if not a probability, that they would prefer to extract some form of spiteful vengeance. The reward for such an amount, if there was one, and if the money was somehow legitimate, would he thought, be both substantial, and negotiable. Ten per cent would give them half a million nearly. That would mean comfort and security, if not actual wealth, for the rest of their lives. It would certainly be better than unemployment benefit, and a council flat. They even dared to dream of a small yacht, or a world cruise. At least a holiday in the sun every year for sure.

The bang on the door made them both panic and jump at the same time. At first Geoffrey wanted to send his wife down the stairs to answer the door, while he waited in the kitchen with a lump hammer in hand. Sanity prevailed as they realised that if it was someone who meant no good, a pregnant woman answering the door might not be any incentive to stop at all. The strange thing with knocks on doors is that they have personalities of their own. There is the timid tap of the unsure, who probably wants to borrow something; the bold confident knock of the door to door salesman, and the religious sect monger. Then there is the officious rap of the police, debt collectors, and irate neighbours. The second hammering of impatient insistence filled them both with dread. Geoffrey crept down the stairs, and called out in a voice that he could not avoid sounding thin, and piping.
'Who is it?'
''Royal Mail sir', the voice said in a military style clip, 'letter to sign for please'.
Geoff was not in the habit of using the door chain, but was extremely grateful that it was fitted. He was also grateful for the frosted glass in the front door, because he could see the broken image of the postman. More importantly, he recognised the man's height, build, and grey hair. It was his regular postie. The letter was from his family abroad, who always registered their mail, in case it went adrift. He undid the chain, quickly opened the door, looked to see that the postman was indeed for real, and rapidly signed something on the bottom line of the form, which was proffered on a clip board.
'No, there if you please', he offered the board again, with the pen poised on the required line, next to the right name. He stared daggers at the unfortunate postman, thinking violent and unkind thoughts.
'Sorry chief, thanks'.
He took the letter and shut the door, bolting it and throwing the latch on the Yale. He latched the chain on too, and went upstairs to Sarah.
'Letter from mum and dad'.
'Oh Christ is that all, I nearly had the baby'.

‘What are we going to do with all this lot? It can't stay here; I will be a nervous wreck by the end of the day’.

He went to the cubby hole, and fetched out the step ladders. In the attic, apart from roof insulation, a T.V. aerial, and cobwebs, were the suitcases for going on holiday. They hadn't been used for nearly four years, and had accumulated old curtains, and blankets, along with other garbage that would 'come in later'. He tipped them out onto the rafters, and handed down the cases. There were only just enough to take the money, after he commandeered his old squash bag, to seconde for the job. He hauled them back up into the roof space, one by one, and closed the wooden hatch. He then buried the steps, back in the cupboard, so that they looked like they hadn't been used for a while. He even thought of shaking the vacuum cleaner bag over them for a dusty effect, but thought that was going a little too far.

Feeling a little safer, they sat to discuss what to do, and still couldn't make their minds up. Half the problem was that they had never found four and a half million quid on the beach before, and lacked the necessary information for dealing with such matters. The immediate instinct was to cut and run. With a few thousand pounds in his wallet, and a wife and two children in tow, especially with her being pregnant, he figured that he could pass as a tourist, just about anywhere. The point was that to go to the banks, was not a safe thing to do. It was obvious that such an amount of money, could not be slipped into a bank account, without at least the tax man being told. The only thing that he could do, was to get the money out of the country as soon as possible. He toyed with the idea of going abroad with some of the money, to open an account. Leaving his wife with four million plus in the attic, was not a healthy thing to do, for her sake. If anything did happen to her and the children, in the two or three days that he would have to be away, he would never forgive himself. No, they were all in together, and safer that way.

He decided on Jersey. It was offshore, the currency was Stirling, and lots of people had offshore money there. He was sure that all of it was not as legitimate as the business world officially led the rest of the country to believe, but then he had always been a cynic. He thought of Liechtenstein, but didn't even know where it is. Switzerland and a numbered account sounded attractive, and so did the Isle of Man. Perhaps after all, it would be better to keep it in bank that he at least knew the name of, and where they spoke English. Jersey he concluded, was the better gamble. In the circumstances, with his family and luggage, it was also probably the easiest to get to. He only had to phone the local airport to book a flight. The other option was the train to Penzance, and either ferry, or scheduled helicopter flight, direct to the Channel Islands. There were no customs to go through from the mainland, as such, and the Brymon Airways flights were just up the road, literally a short taxi ride away. It was the route out which he thought would attract the least attention. All that remained was to organise the trip. He had to make a few phone calls, to the taxi firm, and the airport. To try to arrange to take the children out of school, without attracting too much suspicious attention was the next problem. He thought he could quite successfully invent a lie to pacify the school secretary at least, and their respective teachers could be sold the same line. He decided against contacting any of the banks in advance on the island, better do that from a hotel room when they arrive. All in all he thought his wife and children deserved a break. Then he remembered that airlines do not take heavily pregnant women as passengers. While he reflected on his situation, he saw all the wrappers which were discarded across the kitchen floor. Thinking it too dangerous to just put them in the bin, in case anybody came to snoop his rubbish, he hid the evidence in the roof space with the money. That was the least of his worries, and could be dealt with later. Perhaps he would burn it in the garden later that night. The immediate problem was what to do next. He recognised that he was being pestered by two parasites, hurry, and indecision, both of which can make a mental wreck of anyone who is prone to worry. What he needed was a plan to stick to, and one which can be carried out in secrecy. If there was a clear run, the he would go for the Channel Islands plan after all.

The next tap on the door was a much more friendly and appealing rap. It bore no malice at all. When he opened up to see the blue uniform and pointed helmet of a police constable, his depression was instantaneous.

Chapter Two

Tucked into the back streets of the city of Plymouth, are several cosy public houses. Around The Barbican, and on the East side of Sutton Harbour, in Coxside, several unspoilt Victorian pubs maintain their traditions. The not so traditionally minded, would see them as perhaps a little too 'spit and sawdust' like for their tastes. For those who want a quiet and traditional drink of 'real' ale however, they are a Mecca of authenticity. One place in particular, was frequented by the younger generation. This was not because of any snobbery about the beer that they drank, but because there is live rock music, and some of the customers, were also dealers in drugs. No hard stuff, that anyone was aware of, but a bit of blow on Friday night, didn't seem at all harmful to them. The police, and those members of society, who openly disapprove of youths blowing their impressionable young minds, were seen as so many wet blankets. The arrogance of these young people, who thought that they knew better than those who know better, were going to do their own thing, no matter what the consequences. If they were honest, most of them would have to admit that they chose not to believe the facts. That their activities were both physically, and mentally damaging, was not even part of the equation. What mattered to them was fun, and the pursuit of some Nirvana of happiness. Their beliefs can not be achieved by, but are nonetheless pursued by, the use of mind altering drugs. Any that fall victim to their own addictions, are seen as weak, stupid, or an exception, never the same. Thus the continued use of drugs is perpetuated by the users themselves.

Into such an atmosphere of self centred, and immature, instant gratification, four young men were in their element. They sat in a group, on stools, around a Victorian cast iron table, with a round, solid oak top. They had positioned themselves in the place where they felt most comfortable. In a corner where no-one could come up from behind, without being seen. In a circle, so that each could watch the other's back. They had filled the juke box with money, so that no-one could hear what they said. They were also in silhouette from the window behind, and above. Nobody coming in through the front door, could see who they were. Finally the back door to the yard, was next to the table. If they had been asked, they would have denied that these were the reasons why they sat where they did. Had anyone mentioned the word paranoid, they would probably have been laughed at. If drug addiction were mentioned, they would be gravely insulted. Drug addicts, they asserted, were people who used more, or different drugs than they did.

An average looking man walked into the bar. Denim jacket over a more or less white tee shirt, with blue jeans and a pair of trainers. The international uniform infact, of Mr. Average. One of the four walked over, and talked to him. He nodded yes, and they walked outside together. Five minutes later, they both returned, and continued where they had left off, drinking beer. The drug deal had taken place, without attracting any attention at all. So commonplace was such a transaction these days, that no-one even noticed. Infact they had been more cautious than some. So brazen had the buying and selling of cannabis become, that it often changed hands on top of the table, never mind below it. Of the four Andrew Heslop-Brown was the most ambitious. As his name suggested, if a name is able to suggest anything, he was from what he considered, a middle class background. Somehow he felt, he was superior by right. Not only to his present company in particular, but to the rest of the world in general. He seemed to think that he had a God given right to a comfortable lifestyle. It didn't matter to him, how he came by it, and if the plebes lost all their money to him, by some dishonest practice, that proved him the smarter, and they the inferior trash. He likewise considered his friendship with these others, as a convenience for him to take advantage of, rather than having thought for them.

Lee Arthur Carpenter, Jason William Pengelly, and John Robert Fisher, had been in and out of trouble for most of their short lives. Their stories are much the same in principal, even if they differed in detail. They had played truant from school, and been suspended for fighting and stealing. They were habitual liars, con artists, and thieves. They were motivated by a level of selfish greed, which few are callous enough to sink to. Sitting around their table, they complained about dole money, low standards of living, seedy bedsits, and a general dissatisfaction with life. The only one of them who was in paid employment, was Lee Carpenter. He worked on the assembly line of a printed circuit board factory. It never occurred to them, that a haircut, a collar and tie, and a trip to the local job centre, would do more towards the solution to their problems, than sitting in the pub, complaining about it. Then again, most of them had never done an honest days work in their lives to date, so there was nothing to suggest that they were about to change the habits of a lifetime.

The conversation turned almost inevitably to drugs. They knew that the rewards for taking the risks of smuggling were vast. The trick of course was to avoid customs and excise. Perhaps Jason Pengelly thought that he had something of the smuggler tradition in his Cornish blood, and regarded the act with some kind of twisted romanticism. If fact they all had a romantic impression of running contraband. They saw themselves as later day Crimson Pirates. None remembered Lancaster and Cravat in the least. Heslop - Brown was the most intelligent of the four. At least he was the most ambitious and well connected. Between them, they began to concoct the germ of an idea that would grow into a master plan: To import cannabis resin, from Holland, on a vast scale. It began with the fact that the four of them could sail and navigate. Brown had sailed yachts, and had a master's ticket. He figured that it was about time to put that knowledge into good use. The others had all sailed and crewed to some degree. Apart from Brown, the rest of them had gained their abilities more as a consequence of being beach bums, and hanging around the harbours of the city, than anything else. They had from time to time, been commandeered from the bar, to replace summer crews, who had not turned up for local races and regattas. Over the last few years, they had become quite competent as fair weather sailors. Brown thought that if they could get the money, together with a boat, they could turn over enough to cover their expenses, and turn a handsome profit, in a very short time indeed. The question was how to finance such an undertaking. The answer was already in their pockets. They had just paid twelve pounds for a 'teenth' of cannabis. This amounted to an un-weighed 1\16th part of a 1oz. block. The block would have been cut from a kilogram slab. A 'key' is available for £500. Sold in small quantities to friends, that would return £100 per ounce. At 36 to the kilo, that would return around £36,000 or 720%

Over the next few days, many televisions; car radios, video recorders, cameras, watches, jewellery, and electrical tools and equipment, disappeared from an awful lot of people's homes, garages, and offices. They caught the train to Birmingham, with £3,000 pounds in their pockets. They split up, with two kilograms each, having negotiated 8Kg. for their money. They headed for the Westcountry, to peddle their nasties around the holiday resorts of Devon and Cornwall. They met up back at their local pub, a week later, and called in from there, to Lee's bedsit to count the loot. On account of him being the only one to have work to go to, he stayed at home base. The others drifted from resort to resort, peddling their wares. There was an incredible £28,000, the remainder having been used for frugal expenses. There was now an inevitable argument over the money. None of them had seen so much before. Carpenter, along with Fisher, and Pengelly, were in favour of splitting the cash four ways, and having a good time. Heslop-Brown however, was made of sterner stuff.

If he was lacking in many areas of his personality, like honesty, and common decency, he more than made up for them with tenacity. The others were also, ever so slightly afraid of him. There was one other thing that he possessed, which went beyond daydreaming. He had vision. He had the ability to turn his imagination into a driving force of enthusiasm for others. He was a born leader of men. This was the stuff that gave Adolf Hitler the ability, and drive, to set the crowd alight. This was the burning enthusiasm that lifted him, from a down and out on the streets of Vienna, to the Reich's Fuehrer. Like the war lord, who nearly conquered Europe, Russia, and North Africa, Heslop-Brown was just as bloody crazy about his half-baked ideas, and had just about the same certainty of failure. This drug crazed, arrogant, conceited heap of selfishness, greed, and resentment, was not only going to race in, hell bent for destruction, but was intent on taking others down with him. In his mind, he had already outlined a plan. His intention was to increase his money, ten or twenty fold, and to satisfy his vague dreams, of fast cars, and fast living.

With his master's ticket, and some cash, he could go to a charter company, and hire a yacht for his purposes. With the relevant certificates that he held, and cash up front, he could hire, without suspicion. The story to cover the trip, had to be good enough, but he knew that he could get away with it. By coincidence, one of the staff at FreeMed Yacht Charter, was an acquaintance. They had met on various occasions, at several regattas, and races. A call from the payphone at the bar was all that was required, to arrange an appointment to look over the fleet. For the purposes of sailing across the channel, and the North Sea, in the height of the summer, anything would have fitted his requirements. What this trip needed, was extra bunk space, and a good enough hiding place for the cargo. Brown was insistent on inspecting the overall plan of the vessel. In his mind, he had considered fitting a false bulkhead somewhere. The forward accommodation, or anchor rope well, had been his first idea. A false bottom in the sail locker would fit his needs. If the sails no longer fitted in, then he would lose his Genoa if necessary. There were any number of boats that fitted his needs, and the Westerly 38, was just as good for the purpose, as a Jenneau 36. The extra couple of feet in overall length, made the Westerly slightly more attractive. Whilst weighing up his options, he noticed that Jenneau fitted a 20 gallon fuel tank, and a 62 gallon water tank. He left the charter office for a while, making his excuses, and headed for the local chandlery on the marina.

Within half an hour, he had all the equipment that he needed to hide his illicit load. The best way to hide anything, is to leave it in full view, and disguise it as something else. The very act of changing a floor, or bulkhead, would require a high degree of skill, which he did not personally possess. It would therefore need someone else to know about it, and the less people know, and the fewer of them, the less that can be told. Changing the surface of the woodwork, would need access to matchable veneers, and suitable workshops, which were an unpractical request in the world of sailing. For the most part, people who could afford £80-100,000 for a yacht, had enough money to have a high sense of morality, and honesty. The industry as a whole, from charter companies, to chandlers, is aware of the trade. They are pretty much switched on to the antics of drug traffickers. They tend to report anything suspicious directly to customs. The answer to Heslop-Brown's problem was simplicity itself. It was staring him in the face, just as it would stare anyone who required to search the vessel.

The chandler had supplied him with two lengths of connecting 12m.m. pipe, a couple of junctions, and tee sections to run from the water pump to the galley, and heads. It would all fit in to look like an auxiliary water supply. It was for this reason that he had settled on the charter of the Sundance 36. The forward cabin had a double berth, which measured 2x1 meters, with stowage under the accommodation. There was a vanity unit, next to the bunk, with a hand basin. The collapsible auxiliary water tank, would look neither out of place, nor out of tune, with the original specifications of the vessel.

Having done all of the planning, the rest of the job relied on lists of tasks, and an inventory of their personal needs, over the next few weeks. Whilst he was gaining access to all the equipment, he set the others to task, obtaining other requirements. The lists seemed endless. Apart from all the food, clothing, and the first aid kit, they needed extra flares, life jackets, and storm weather gear. The watches needed to be organised. Charts had to be bought, and courses plotted. Nothing was left to chance. Knowing that the least reliable of the crew, was Lee Carpenter, he set him the most ordinary, but nonetheless equally important of the tasks. Carpenter knew little of the equipment, and was the least experienced of the four, in either sailing, or crime. One of his tasks, was to go and buy, specifically from two different shops, some black plastic bin liners, and tape to wrap them with, when they were used. The bags were bought in a supermarket, and some parcel tape from an ironmonger's store. Not leaving these most important items to chance, Heslop-Brown decided on a test run. He filled a bag with newspapers, and wrapped them up in three plastic bags. The whole lot was sealed up with parcel tape, and dumped in the bath.

The problem with sailing the high seas is the damp. No matter how well built the boat, and no matter how careful the skipper, eventually everything becomes damp. In really bad weather, it is impossible to keep even the least bit dry. Everything is cold and clammy to the touch. That was the reason for the bath test. The very last thing that they wanted was having tonnes of very expensive drugs, soaked through with sea water. The result was a disaster. The news papers were thoroughly soaked, into a soggy mess of papier mache, which was of no use to man nor beast. The bags were waterproof enough; after all, they were made of polythene, a total water barrier. The problem it seemed was the tape. After a few hours in the water, the glue turned into an opaque film, and it no longer seemed to stick to the bags. Parcel tape is designed for use on dry goods, and for sealing, and holding, cardboard boxes together. In its proper use, it is second to none. The adhesive however, was not designed for use with polythene, and infact, doesn't stick too well at all to the smooth surface. In an inspiration of lateral thinking, the up to the moment dull, and uninspired Carpenter, had a flash of inspiration. He was employed on the production line of a printed circuit board manufacturer. The only thing that he had done in his youth that was of value today in his work was to twang on his guitar. It was not as if he had musical talent, or the ability to tear a riff off the strings. He had gained as a matter of secondary co-incidence, some considerable dexterity. This enabled him to find employment, on the production line, putting printed circuit boards together.

As part of the production process of circuit boards, after all the electrodes have been soldered to the boards, they have to be gold plated. In order to carry out this process accurately, and without over plating the circuits, in places that will cause problems, the individual parts are masked off. It is necessary that the tape performs in a predictable way, seals well, and is easy to remove when the plating process is finished. This very special tape, is manufactured especially for the industry, and Sellotape plating mask tape, sticks very well to plastics. Carpenter simply slipped a roll into his pocket, on the way past the storeroom, and took the roll for his partner in crime to try.

They wrapped a toilet roll, in a plastic carrier bag, and sealed it up with the tape. It floated in the bath like a rubber duck. The next morning it was still afloat. They ripped it open, to find the tissue bone dry underneath. Having found the experiment a success, Carpenter stole another two rolls of plating tape, so that they would be certain that there was enough for the job. He added them to the increasing amount of stores, piling up in Heslop-Brown's flat. There was barely enough room to move in there, let alone to live and sleep. The time had come to make a move. Probably the fastest way to attract attention, when chartering yachts, or buying Rolls Royces, is to walk into the salesman's office, to sign the order form, with a briefcase full of cash, to pay upfront. This is what Brown intended to do, but thought better of it. Opening bank accounts in false names, to pay by cheque, is just as risky. In the end, he opted for a sob story, with a dribble of cash, at regular intervals.

People will not be prepared to tolerate the arrogance of walking into their office, with cash up front, when the buyer looks like he is on the dole. A sob story, with a decent deposit on the other hand, works every time. No-one likes to see a grown man cry. With this in mind, he went back to Free-Med, and opened up with an apology for not being able to conclude their business earlier. His excuse was that he had to speak with his father, on the telephone first. With the resigned look, of the salesman who had seen it all before, the agent said that he understood. In his mind, he wished that young people, with parents who had too much money, would fall flat on their faces occasionally. Instead of which, the inevitable 'phone call to daddy' was always needed, and they were always bailed out. He still wasn't quite sure if he was jealous because he did not have a rich family, or in despair at their shallow dependence upon their parents. In truth he had felt the discomfort of being lied to, and had not quite connected, because he didn't trust his own instincts.

The Jenneau Sunfast 36, is an exceptionally beautiful craft, its sharp lines, and sleek racing trim, make it a design dream; of style, luxury, and nerve tingling, elegant beauty. To the sailor on the helm, the yacht feels alive. It has a personality, and an individual entity, like the spirit of a thoroughbred race horse. She is in fact classy, French, sexy, looks it and feels it. Brown handed over £500 as a deposit, with a fawning apology over the delay in payment. The rest he assured would arrive tomorrow. The next day, he walked in with £600, which paid for a week's charter. The master's certificate secured the keys, and he went to borrow a van, to begin to load. Being ever cautious of the mistake of being conspicuous on the one hand, and furtively suspicious on the other, they loaded the yacht quietly over three days. Brown then went into the charter office, and paid for another two weeks of hire. At the end of the third afternoon, the boat was moored up at the marina dock, with an excuse of problems with the water. He insisted that he could manage, if he had a day to work on the pump.

The forward berth lifted up to reveal the bunk stowage underneath. Removing the inspection hatch to the forward water tank, he gained access to the pipe work. The flexible hose of the vanity unit sink, was easy to slice through with a sharp knife. A tee piece, which he had bought in the chandlery shop, was blocked off, with a small rubber bung, to seal it, and his new section of hose, slipped over the top. From the outside, it looked like a working joint, but flow was stopped by the bung. Switching the pump on, and trying the sink, and shower, confirmed that there were no leaks. Replacing the inspection plate, the pipe passed into the space under the forward accommodation. In this 2x1 metre space, a collapsible auxiliary water tank, was put into the bunk, and to anything but a fully destructive inspection, it looked normal.

The interior of the water tank, had taken a little longer to prepare. The filler for the tank, was an outer 'female' ring, sealed into another 'male' ring, with a neoprene washer. The employment of a pair of Stilson wrenches, with their jaws wrapped in rag, had separated the joint, without scoring the outer ring. It looked as though it had not been touched. A strong polythene bag was fitted into the collapsible tank. When the tank, was later filled with drugs, the bag would take about five gallons of water. The whole thing was trimmed to fit the outer ring. The addition of the neoprene washer, and the inner ring, would make it waterproof. The tank appeared serviceable, and could even be inspected, by taking off the filler cap, and seeing the water inside the inner sleeve. Unless there was a definite search, it would pass any border inspection.

The whole boat was ready to go. The time had come to finalise his financial deal with his contact, and get the show on the road. He left the yacht, and walked up to the telephone box in the marina, then he called a taxi. He was on his way to report to the man who had filled his mind, over the last couple of weeks, and unknown by the others, was paying for the entire finance of the trip. It was Thursday evening, and they were ready to sail on Friday, as was agreed with his financier. They were about to begin the consummation of their wildest dreams.

Chapter Three

At last the end of the shift was in sight. Police constable Grayson, was not the career type. He had joined the force to be a policeman, and there was not a lot about the promotional ladder, that was remotely attractive to him. The idea of a fast track career, to climb the ladder, left him colder than a plunge pool in a sauna bath. The things that he was good at were fact crunching, list reading and the comparison of statements. If there were two lists of names, which to most people were identical, Grayson would spot the changed initial, or miss-spelt surname, faster than most. He had a knack to spot the odd, and a tenacity to explain the mysterious. He was very good indeed at police work. The only thing he did not like about the job, was (as he saw it), the unnecessary mountain of bureaucratic paperwork. It sometimes seemed to hinder more than help, in solving crime. For that reason alone, he had never sat his sergeant's examinations. His peers thought that he would make detective inspector, if he wanted to. He didn't want to. As was his usual habit, just before he handed over his shift, he took out his little book. Now this was not his official pocket book. The entries were not so much notes, as niggles, and observations from the day - The car with road grit gathering underneath, and dirty windows. Why had it not been moved? He knew as well as anyone else that it had not been reported stolen. He had checked. He had checked who the car was registered to, and that it was parked in the right street. It had a current road fund licence. The car was not old as such, and appeared to be well maintained. The niggle was why it had not been used. The owner could simply be on holiday, but he put it in his little book. There was a flat, in King Street. The curtains had been drawn for two days. Again there is nothing wrong with that, but nonetheless, it was odd, and it went in the book.

Under just such an entry, was the Lada Riva, which he had noted on his way into the station, not half an hour ago. The fact was that there had been nothing wrong, and that was the problem. People who drive at thirty miles an hour, or more precisely, twenty-nine miles per hour, at six o'clock in the morning, did not want to attract attention to themselves. It was true that he drove up behind, and if the driver was awake, then he would know that there was a police car up his exhaust pipe. The niggle was that he had tried the man's mettle, by driving just a yard too close for coincidence. The result was that there had been no speeding up, or slowing down for that matter. And that was the problem. It was all just too neat, so it went in the jotting pad. Back at the station, in the canteen, he went over the day with the rest of the shift. It came up in conversation, that someone had picked up some parcels, off the beach at Devil's Point, and drove off in a Lada.

To overstate the obvious connection, would be an insult to Grayson's intelligence. He immediately informed his sergeant, who made the necessary call up on the computer. He handed Wilson's name and address over, before anyone had finished their tea. In view of the suspicious circumstances, of possible smuggling, it was decided to make an immediate call on the house. At this stage, as there was no drug related record from criminal records office, a softly, softly approach was used. One police car was parked in the street, and the two officers went to knock on the door. Just in case, there was a Ford Transit mini-bus, waiting around the corner. In it were half the police force rugby football team. P.C. Grayson accompanied by a woman police officer, because there was a woman, and children in the flat, approached the door. Officer Grayson gently tapped on the door, using the letter box flap. There were footfalls down a wooden staircase, and the clatter of bolts, chains, and a lock being thrown back. The two officers exchanged glances at the amount of security being unhitched. They knew they were on to something, when the thirty something man opened the door, looked out, and almost fainted at the sight of the police. His face went that ashen grey of the guilty, and his expression moved from curious to furious, in about a tenth of a second.

'Mr. Wilson!'
It was more of a statement than a question. Geoffrey Arthur Wilson, had been around long enough to know, that the copper on the doorstep, knew very well who he was.
'Yes'
'I am P.C. Grayson, and this is P.C. McAlister. Can we come in Mr. Wilson?'
He attempted the usual stalling tactics, which were quickly countered.
'Well we don't want your neighbours to hear do we?'
Geoffrey was still too nonplussed, to think of saying that there was not a neighbour in sight, let alone within hearing distance. He crumbled, and allowed the officers in.
'Have you been out this morning Mr. Wilson?'
He lied. It was expected.
'You were out with your dog this morning, on the beach, at Devil's point.'
There was no point in lying any longer. He allowed himself just a little justification to save face, and further embarrassment.
'Well yes. I walked the dog that is all. I haven't been anywhere as such'.
'Mr. Wilson'. He affected a patronising, and condescending tone of voice, as if speaking to a naughty boy. 'You were seen this morning, in the early hours, at Devil's Point'' Grayson had added 'in the early hours', to make it sound suspicious. He then rubbed it in, by deliberately flipping, his black official note book out, and studiously consulted it, before going any further.
'You were seen to load several packages, which you had brought up from the sea front, into your car, and speed away', he dramatised.
'Yes I did pick up several bin liners full of gash. I put them with the other piles, outside the night clubs in Union Street. I should not be surprised, if it was not all down at Chelson Meadow tip by now, where it belongs'.
He added the 'where it belongs', to counter the 'suspicious', and 'speed away' jibes.
'You would be better off chasing yachties, for gashing their crap over the side, instead of dealing with it properly. If it

wasn't for me, and others like me, who use the beach on a regular basis, the whole place would be awash with rubbish bags. And further more,...'
'Thank you Mr. Wilson'.

The Saint Citizen line was lost on Grayson, and McAlister for that matter. They exchanged glances again. This time, the unspoken message, that this man was lying through his back teeth, was unmistakably noted by both of them.
'In that case Mr. Wilson, you won't mind if we have a quick look around the flat then will you'.

Grayson began to make a move, to look behind the sofa. He didn't hold much hope of finding anything there. He didn't think he would find anything of much worth, if he turned the place over. Like the rest of the three piece suite, the settee was brown, dowdy, and had the persona of the second hand social security standard. The whole flat had the depressing air of seediness, that is the inheritance of the poor. The yellowing paintwork, was in dire need of a new coat of gloss. The wallpaper should have been changed two years ago. The whole place infact, had the air of the unemployed, whose income was not that of anyone, up to anything that they shouldn't be.
'Yes as it happens, I would mind very much'.
'Well if you have nothing to hide Mr. Wilson, I cannot see what your objection could possibly be'.
'There are two objections constable. The first is that there is nothing to find. The second is that I would hate to see Her Majesty's time and money wasted.'
'We could always get a warrant'.
P.C. Grayson imagined the wrath of the magistrate, when asked to supply a warrant. To want to search the flat of a public spirited citizen, who had simply picked up some rubbish, and put it in the right place for disposal. If this man was telling the truth, then he would look a right berk. It was also obvious, that this Mr. Wilson had some experience, or at least had been interviewed by the police before. He had thought of trumping something up as a softener. He considered the possibilities for a few seconds longer, and in a moment of indecision, thought of

running Wilson in. It lasted no longer than a moment. The way to get to the bottom of this mystery was surely to be absolutely sure of the facts, before asking any more questions. There were going to be a few hours of cat and mouse chess moves, where the first one to make a mistake would undoubtedly lose. Both parties understood this stand-off, and the importance of playing the game by the rules. The way things had gone so far, he thought Wilson would sit in the cell, with impassive patience. In the interview room, he would probably not be intimidated by the pressure of the tape recorder. He would as likely as not, listen to his caution, and take it literally. A tape full of 'I have nothing to say thank you', would be of little to no use at all. Constable Grayson was too good at his job, and too experienced to alienate Wilson at this stage.
'Very well Mr. Wilson, that will be all for now, but we may be back later. I am going to make further enquiries, and if I cannot verify your story, I will be back. I can assure you of that'.
'Thank you officers, good morning to you'. He refused to bite.
In the car outside, Grayson and McAlister compared notes, or more specifically feelings. They both agreed on almost all points that they covered. That Wilson was lying; they were in no doubt of. That there was more to this than meets the eye, they agreed upon. That Wilson was afraid of something, more frightening than the police, was odds on favourite. At that point they split into two distinct and differing camps.

McAlister was more in favour of the most obvious and cynical explanation. Her theory was that this man was out of work, and out of luck. He had a wife, two children, and the imminent arrival of another child, to support and worry about. He was living in an overcrowded and rented council flat, which was a better place to move from than to. She believed that he had been given the opportunity to take a risk. To collect someone's drugs from the beach, and deliver them to their distribution point, for a handsome pay cheque. She was all for calling in Customs and Excise, who did not need a warrant to search. She would arrest the whole household, and call in social services, to look after the kids, and turn the place over there and then.

Grayson had an idea that things were not as bad as that, but that something was going on, that he did not have the answer to yet. He had the notion that Wilson was not so much lying, as not telling the whole truth in part, and misleading with deliberate lies, in other areas of his story. He believed for instance, that the reason for going to the beach, was genuinely to walk the dog. He believed that his suspect had found something, maybe even drugs. He did not believe the eyewash about cleaning up the beach, because of some sense of public duty. He would have left it by the bins in the car park, not load them into his car, and drive off with them. So there remained two questions. What was in the bags? and how to catch his man? He picked up the radio handset, and keyed the transmit button. The sergeant, who trusted Grayson's judgement implicitly, agreed to leave a car, parked a safe enough distance away not to arouse attention, and in plain enough view of the premises, to monitor all movements.

After the police had gone, Sarah breathed a sigh of relief that they had bought a little time. Neither she nor her husband, were naive enough, to think that this was the end of it, or that they had managed to deter the police so easily. They knew that they were being played. Geoffrey watched out of the landing window, which rather successfully, looked down pretty much of the street. He was a little surprised to see the mini bus full of coppers, pulling out of the next street, and driving away. He began to realise, that if he had made any moves to resist the two gentle officers, the heavy mob were just around the corner, waiting for a call on the radio. He was less surprised to see an unmarked saloon pull up, just up the street. Its two passengers did not get out. They were still there ten minutes later.

Now the Wilsons had a philosophy in life. It was their contention that if you break your leg, you don't go to the newsagent to ask for advice. Nor do you put a sticky plaster on the break, and hope it will go away. They were deep in the compost, and could not see a way to worm out of it alone. When in legal difficulties, call a lawyer. When he picked up the phone to make the call, he was tempted to ask for advice on the 'green form' scheme. This would give him half an hour or so of legal advice, on the legal aid scheme. In view of the amount of cash in the attic, he thought that this would be taking the Mickey a little bit too much. He was unable to explain too much on the telephone. He had a vague suspicion, that this was no longer a safe line. When he tried to entice the solicitor out of his nice warm office, he encountered some trouble. When he explained that he could not call into the office, because he was besieged by policemen, who were watching his flat, the lawyer was interested. When the idea that the entire family might be in some considerable trouble was relayed, he was intrigued. On the promise of a steaming mug of fresh ground coffee, he agreed to come at once. Geoff wondered if the man would need to be bribed with coffee, if he had said that he had just committed some heinous crime of violence.

Watching the road, as the solicitor's car pulled up outside, the wide angled lens camera was swung into action as soon as he got out of the car. The police were being thorough and none too subtle about it either. If they were trying to apply pressure, he could assure them that it was working. When the Moulinex had gurgled its stuff, and the flat was filled with the warm aroma of fresh coffee, they sat down at the kitchen table, and Geoffrey Wilson began to relate his tale to the now amazed solicitor. After twenty minutes or so of listening very carefully to what was being said, and taking down notes on his A4 pad, council sat up, and began to report, as he saw it, the law as it stands. He also began to ask more precise details, of the exact location of the errant bags.

'I want to ask you some questions, and clear up one or two points before we go any further, and then we can see what is to be done. Where are the bags now?'

'Up in the attic'.

'And have you counted it all? Are you sure of the precise amount?'

'Well we counted it. I counted it, and Sarah checked it. We marked down the number of thousands on sheets. Here you are, here are the sheets we used to count it.'

‘So you marked off a single stroke for each thousand, and crossed off very five. I take it that the two columns gives ten thousand for each line.’

‘Yes and there is £4,521,375, as exactly as I can tell.’

‘Very well, firstly it is vitally important that you account for all of the money. Have you been tempted to put a few thousand pounds on one side, before calling me?’

‘As it happens, no. We had kind of decided to keep all of it. Until the police arrived that is’.

‘Just as well you did. You might have made a serious error, which would have put you in serious trouble. If a claimant comes along, and knows the exact amount of money there, it is important that there is none hidden away. Now explain to me again, exactly where you found the money’.

‘It was just like I said. I was walking the dog, and there they were, lying at the top of the paddling pool, at the top of the beach’.

‘Now this is very important, and I want you to think very carefully before you answer. Were these bags actually lying on the top of the shingle, on the beach, or were they in the pool?’

‘Well both really’.

‘Well it cannot be both, so I would stay with the shingle description, rather than the pool, if I were you. You see if they were floating in the pool proper, there may be an argument that they were found on council property. Though it could be argued that, that particular piece of construction, being in part a natural part of the strand in situ, could give rise to a prima facie case that...'

‘Hold on a minute. What does that all mean?’

‘Sorry. The construction of the pool can be seen as part of the erosion barrier, as much as the pool proper. Part of it just slopes down as a section of the beach. Anyway the whole thing is at the mercy of the tide. If I recall, it does lie between the high and low water marks doesn’t it?’

‘Well yes, but that's the whole point of it surely.’

‘Yes but you see, at the top of the beach, there is no wall or construction is there? It blends in with the rest of the beach,

along with the sea wall, and the steps down from the erosion barrier'.
'So'.
'The point is Mr. Wilson, if the packages were just lying on the sand, it makes all the difference. Oh yes. They were not buried in any way, or concealed, or hidden were they?'
'No'.
'Good. Then as far as I can tell, under treasure trove law, the money belongs to you.'
'What do you mean, belongs to me? Do you mean all this police hassle is for nothing? That they have no rights to hound me like this?'
'No Mr. Wilson, I mean that because you have not been exactly forward with them, and have been economical with the truth, to say the least, they are not satisfied with your answers. They still want answers, and who can blame them? They may well think that you have collected a considerable haul of drugs, even if you did just happen to find them. You and I both know, that if you did find such a haul, you would take them straight to the police station, and hand them in, but they don't. I would say that if you do not contact them, by say the end of the day, they may claim that you have wasted police time, at the very least. They would have a little difficulty in making it stick, but you would become a very public figure, and in view of your find, I do not think that you would want that somehow.

To come back to the main point - The only parties who have a claim on the find are; The Crown, if it can be shown to be treasure trove, the landowner, if the money was found on private land, the person who originally lost the money of course, and yourself. I quickly looked up an interpretation of the treasure trove laws, before I left the office. It states quite clearly that, 'any money or coin, gold, silver, plate, or bullion, that is found hidden in the earth, or in any other secret place, belongs to The Crown, by prerogative right. It does state quite clearly though, that The Crown gains no title, (or has no right to it, if you like), unless the money is actually hidden in the earth, with the intention of recovering it. In this instance it would seem, that is the case - That the money was not hidden'.

‘Yes but...’

The solicitor held up his hand, in a gesture that prevented interruption.

‘Hold on, it gets better, The person who lost it has a right to it, if he is known, or afterward discovered, if they can show that it was hidden, and clearly it was not hidden, but lost. Now then, the definition also quite clearly states that, and quite specifically,...where it is scattered in the sea, or on the surface of the earth, or lost, or abandoned, it belongs to the first finder. It goes on a bit, to reinforce the fact that The Crown has first refusal if it was hidden, but only if someone else cannot show a better title. I think you may well be able to show, that you are the one, in this instance, who has the better title. Now I am not a gambling man, but I would not like to lay odds on the probability, that the person who lost the money, would not have the courage to march into the local nick, and lay claim to it. There are going to be some very awkward questions indeed. Like where it came from? Why is it being moved like this? Let alone the tax and V.A.T. that may be owed on it. I know it will be difficult to do, but this is my best advice. Take the money into the police station. We will phone first, and have security set up. Hand the money over to the lost property counter. I will come with you, to make sure that you receive your lost property ticket correctly. We will ensure that the money gains proper interest on your behalf, whilst it is in police custody. I will stay with you in case they wish to interview you. I have no doubt that they will. You will have to chew your nails for ninety days, but in the end the money will be legally yours. You will not have to look over your shoulder for the rest of your lives. If the worst happens, and the original owner does turn up to claim his property, then you will be entitled to a finders fee, of say 20%, legal costs, and possibly the interest on all of the money since the day you found it. That should amount to nearly a million in itself, which is not a bad payout for a morning's work is it?’

Geoffrey and Sarah Wilson could not believe their ears. All that worry was just for the sake of doing what he was going to do in the first place, but for his greed.

As the phone call was made, they felt their fears slip away. The knowledge that no matter what happens now, nobody is going to end up with the stress of having to appear before the courts. They were sure that even if they were not going to be able to retain the vast fortune in the attic, they were going to be rich by most standards. In comparison to the drudgery of existence on state benefits, they would be positively wealthy from the finder's fee alone. His calculator told him that he should collect £904,275 at least.

'Sarah my dear, I think you can throw out that pram we bought, and you can have a brand new one, from wherever you wish, Harrods if you like.'

'Don't you think that it would be better to give it to someone less fortunate than us? and buy one more modestly?'

'Well love, it's like the saw isn't it. Finders Keepers and all that'.

Their arrival at the police station was accompanied by a security truck. The security officers themselves went up into the attic, with steel cases. They packed all the cash up and loaded it, one at a time, through the armour plated cash chute. The contrast was vivid to the way it arrived, in the boot of a Lada Riva, in black plastic bags.

Once the whole story had been told, the police were more than satisfied, that in interview room 3, were a very lucky couple. The duty inspector was very much concerned for the safety of the finders. There was a good possibility that there was someone in town, who was looking for the people who had handed their money in to the police. If his guess was right, he doubted that they would try to recover it, through the county court. He decided that they would take the unusual step, of having the identity of the finders kept secret. The officers involved were sworn to silence, and no press release was allowed. Just to seal up any gaps, .P.C. McAlister was dispatched to Susan Birch's flat, whose telephone call had started all of this in the first place. She was told that she had seen, a public minded citizen, disposing of some bags of rubbish, which had washed up on the beach. She elaborated to say, that the vessel concerned with the dumping of waste in The

Sound, had been traced, and was to be prosecuted. She was sure that if this public snoop got the message that blood was to be drawn, she would let it drop. Just in case the Wilson's lost the property ticket, as if that were likely, the receipt was handed in for safe keeping in the vault safe, of the solicitor's bankers. They would collect it in ninety days. The money was in the bank, all of it that is, except for a few sample notes, from each parcel. They would be examined later for forensic evidence.

All of them had been given the once over, under ultra violet light. Marks and finger prints showed up, and these were retained for later examination. The original bags, and their wrappings, were also retained. They were bagged up, and packed for dispatch to the forensic laboratories, where they would be thoroughly examined, for any evidence of their origin, and any traces that would give a clue to the identity of the owner, or handlers of the money. There was no solid, or for that matter, even remotely useable evidence, on the surface of the notes themselves. There was the occasional smudge, but nothing that was going to satisfy the requirements of a court. The only hope was that there was some evidence in the wrappings. To most people, bin bags were bin bags. They were all made by someone, using differing materials, techniques, and manufacturing processes, which made them to a degree, identifiable. There was one piece of evidence, an unfortunate oversight, in Heslop-Brown's so far immaculate planning, which led almost directly to him.

Chapter Four

Of the people who are successful in business, if success is measured in salaries, there are two distinct stereotypes. The careers orientated are one group, and the self made success stories are the other. The differences between them are so striking, that they contrast to the point, where there is no similarity between them. They are born into different lifestyles, and are brought up to, and live by, different moral standards. The top few percentage of the population, who have annual incomes that make most people's lifetime salaries pale into small change, arrive there by two distinct paths. It is true that for most, they are neither completely one type, nor the other. It is also true to say, that there are some, who have high power, and vast incomes, because of who they are, rather than what they know. These people are mostly harmless, because they employ others, who have the experience and skill, to make day to day working decisions, on their behalf. It may well be, that the public school, and red brick university educated, have ingrained into them, a deep sense of moral responsibility, and self worth. They value people, and have standards that are sacrosanct. The other extreme of the scale, is occupied by a very few people indeed. Their motive in life, is entirely dedicated, to the accumulation of wealth and power. They do not care who they damage, or destroy to gain their ends. They have no consideration for anyone. They do not care if their business dealings cause harm; death, destruction, famine, homelessness, and degradation. At their very worst, they don't even ask themselves if their practices are within the law.

Denis Weatherfield was one of these. Like others of his sort, he was probably jealous of others. He believed that he should have been sent to Harrow, Rugby, or even Eton College. In fact he was an average product, of an average state school.

His education and social circles left him with an affinity toward soccer, Led Zeppelin, and darts. He was in his late twenties when he began to mix with, and be aware of people who read Shakespeare, went to the opera, and enjoy poetry, fine art, and more importantly, fine living. Weatherfield began to look upon the trappings of the rich and famous, not as a fact for them, and a goal in life for him, but as a personal right. Wealth became an obsession. He was a simple tradesman in the construction industry, and his greed fed his motivation to amass more, and as quickly as possible. He began to take risks. Courage and determination were qualities he did not lack. He used them to the utmost. In a few short years, he had expanded from a one man business, to a medium sized company. The firm employed a hundred or more people, administering contracts of ever increasing size. He had been lucky in some respects, and he would be the first to admit it.

By being in the right place at the right time, he had managed to close deals on prestigious projects. He had invested in property wisely too. He had bought unattractive land cheaply, only to find in a very short time, that because of the changes in use, in certain properties down the road, his bomb sites became gold mines. His games of golf; lunches, dinners, night clubs, and 'hostess' dates, with a certain man in the planning office, who happened to be married, had nothing to do with it of course.

One of his other tricks, which is particularly nasty, is worming his way out of paying the workforce. There were two ways in which he did this. Firstly he would award a contract of minor worth, to a small tradesman. The small and struggling builder, thinking that his day in business had arrived, and receiving the contract for the work, eagerly signed it and awaited the day to begin work. On arrival on site, he would be asked if he would do a little extra job. Eager to please, he employs extra men to do the work. The more he does, the more he is awarded. At the end of the job, he hands in his bill, and is paid for the original contract only. Upon complaint, he is told that he has contracted to work for a fixed price, for which he has been paid. The small tradesman is now owed ten times the amount that he is going to be paid for. He cannot even meet the wages bill, let alone his suppliers. With his rapacious creditors hammering on the back door, and his bankers and employees on the front, he has no choice but to collapse. In a state of insolvency, he loses his home, his business, and possibly even his family under the strain. Some even take their own lives, under the unbearable mental stress. Weatherfield on the other hand, is forced to buy another Mercedes, in order to avoid paying the extra profits out to the Inland Revenue. The final sickening touch to this malicious plot, is to send a quantity surveyor, and site agent to the job, to 'discover faults' with the work. He then falsifies the 'repair' invoices, for rectifying work, by trades companies that actually belong to himself. The fictitious work is then counter charged to the contractor. The duped tradesman then ends up actually in debt to The Weatherfield organisation.

Another method that he employed, the second of his two way system, was an insurance against the first not working. At the outset of a new main contract, and at the negotiation stages with the client, he made himself personally involved. What he did not tell his clients, or his main sub-contractors, was that he was merely an employee of the company, contracted as a consultant. When it went broke, he was not only the main profiteer, but to the outside world, was one of the losing contractors. He ended up owing himself a few thousand pounds, which he could write off against tax as a bad debt. His contracts were inevitably with a shell company. The three share, off the shelf firm, was specifically bought, and set up to be the main contractor. His company were employed as sub-contractors of the shell company. When the manure hit the fan, all of the assets of the shell company, were paid to Weatherfield's contracting company, as bona fide payments, for services rendered. The limited liability of the firm, when the liquidator was called in, was the princely sum of £3. Everyone else, more or less, walked off with empty pockets, ruined businesses, and ruined lives. The money of course, was allocated offshore, months previously, and not only did nobody but Weatherfield win, but he was fireproof too. He had done nothing that was actually illegal. What was amazing, was that he was able to sleep at night.

The one all important, and abiding rule that Weatherfield never broke, was never to swindle anyone who had the remotest chance of gaining revenge, either by fair means or foul. For this reason, and because he was very much aware that to keep things going to need allies, he bribed his way into every official channel that he could. With this came the reputation among accountants, solicitors, architects, and town planners alike, that Denis Weatherfield's' parties were the best in town. His entertainment was both lavish, and frequent. There had been more than one minor official, whose election to the golf club, and other elitist social circles, had springboard their careers. They were left in no doubt either, that the reason for their swift promotions, were entirely down to the generosity of Weatherfield. They also knew that these gifts, and assistance, had a pay-day in the future, of unknown value. Many people over the years, by one favour or another, were firmly in the pocket of Denis Weatherfield. At one of his wild parties, he had been asked for his advice, on tight lipped staff, by a man who had lost out on a controversial job. The story was that a direct drainage plan, which would have resulted in a raw sewage discharge, was blocked. Somehow information was leaked, and an environmental lobby, with the aid of some well-timed press releases, stopped the planning application from being successful. Weatherfield of course knew just the man for the job. He had just passed his examinations, for The Institute of Secretaries and Administrators. He was well qualified for a senior post, and came highly recommended. A mutual arrangement was made to introduce the two parties, and the problem was apparently solved.

What wasn't said was that the man worked for Weatherfield. There had been some problem to do with the misappropriation of funds, a few years ago. Weatherfield helped dig the man out of the hole, with a little money, and legal assistance. He also paid for the tuition and examination fees. Yet another professional was on the payroll, and in debt. The investment was now about to pay back with interest. He had his man on the inside of a company, upon which he would soon start to prey. The golden egg of this particular fatted goose was Europe. Among the areas of trade that were attractive at the moment, were building works in Eastern Europe. With the unification of Germany, the whole of what was East Germany, was wide open for investment, and development, and that meant both demolition, and construction.

With the collapse of the Soviet Bloc, it was possible that up to one third of the land mass of the planet, had opened up as a new market place. The potential was mind blowing. Within a few months of having his man in place, Weatherfield began to receive reports of the construction of a new factory, for a German pharmaceutical company, in the old Eastern sector of Berlin. Not only did the information of who the clients were, by name, come to his notice, copies of the tenders and their prices also landed on his desk at the same time. The undercut on the quote was fixed and in place with the clients within the week. A few faxes, and a fortnight later, saw him on a flight to Berlin, to close the deal. Whilst in Berlin, he took a few days off to see the sights, as well as looking at areas in which he could operate within the city. It seemed like a ripe plum, ready for the picking.

At his hotel one evening, he shared an hour, and a vodka, with a man who was a fellow guest. A chemist as it turned out, who was impatient it seemed, for the new factory to begin production. It is one of the prices of free enterprise, that employment by the state is no longer guaranteed. When the state no longer exists, the secret research and development, of many Government sponsored projects, cease to exist with them. Mass redundancy was right across the board, with chemists, physicists, botanists, geneticists, and all manner of scientific bakers and candlestick makers, finding themselves in redundant occupations. Over the hour, the scale of the well-reported corruption in Eastern Europe became more apparent. The scrabble from the restraints of communism, was proving painful. One day there was a small flat, a low wage, and the state allocation of privileges. The next there was the freedom to work, and earn all that the individual was capable of achieving.

To draw a comparison with Red Indians and Redeye, would be understandable. With the beginnings of raw trade, came instant profits. If these were small to begin with, at least they had the advantage of being in cash. Like all cash trade, it is difficult, if not impossible to regulate accurately. There was a sudden and ever widening gap, between the haves and the have nots. In this case, some of those who were being left out, were the very people who were meant to regulate it. Trade was becoming a crazed gold rush, with greed overtaking sanity. The more barriers were dropped, and opportunities were opened up with the west, the more the black market expanded. The more it expanded, the more it fed upon itself. The graft that was being paid to officials to turn their backs, spread even wider. Corruption was now so rife, that very little moved without a back hander being paid.

It was inevitable that this mayhem of a feeding frenzy, should attract the bigger sharks. When the social cancer of organised crime began to infect, and spread through the naive and new-born society, it robbed the child of its innocence with brutal force. In this atmosphere Denis Weatherfield saw much more opportunity than he had seen previously. The only links missing in the chain were the connections, the vehicle to make profit, and the method of operating a lucrative import, export business. His first fleeting idea was to send over denim jeans, and jackets. This was not only bulky, but had been done before. He could also see a great loss of stock, to the many people who would have to handle the goods. He decided to have a further chat with his chemist friend. Perhaps Western pharmaceuticals could be imported, but what to export. With that kind of fateful coincidence, that throws like minded people together, the man in the bar was about to form a new relationship. It was to become a business partnership, of such vast profitability, that it would almost defy thinking about.

Over the next couple of days, it became clear that the chemist, and two of his friends, were still plying their trade. Without an employer or a laboratory to work in, they had set up a crude factory, in a flat at the top of a tenement block, manufacturing amphetamine sulphate, or speed. It was also clear that these over qualified drug pushers, were capable of much more, if they had the equipment to do it. They needed a legitimate cover, and a laboratory to manufacture their wares. They assured him that they were capable of making designer drugs like ecstasy. They explained that by looking up the chemical methylenedioxymethamphetamine, in something like a copy of Merck Index, the constituent chemicals, and method of manufacture, could simply be looked up. They went further to say, that the reduction of benzylmethyl keytone in ethanol and sulphuric acid, will produce amphetamine. If they rearranged the molecules with an alcohol molecule, the result would be ecstasy rather than just straight speed.

In the ordinary run of affairs, it was easy to cover the illicit hardware. The trusted western businessman, with a contract to build a chemical plant, had no trouble at all in organising and importing the glassware and goods, with which to set up a bootleg factory. The basic constituents they found to be as readily available, as any other industrial requirements. In the paperwork, should anyone care to inspect it, were certain small write offs. In a major building contract, of such a size and proportion, there are bound to be losses of material. There always has been, and always will be, theft of small tools and materials, from building sites. Where this is controlled as much as possible, it is impossible to eradicate completely. There is always accidental loss, from breakage, handling, and the mistakes made by fallible people. This is never really detailed in accounting, except as a predictable percentage. As long as the losses stay within the limits set down by the accountant, then nobody really takes much notice. In any case, even if attention were paid to such losses, it is doubtful if much could be traced, without a massive, and very expensive investigation. The cost of recovery would exceed the value of the loss. This is the conundrum which makes the crooks' dream. In order to make the apparent unmanageability acceptable, a euphemism is used. Theft and carelessness become simply, and more acceptably, the word shrinkage. In a few short weeks, a steady local trade had been set up. This expanded into a sizeable domestic operation in designer drugs. All the people who needed to profit from it were doing so, and the tragic results of taking ecstasy were already happening.

In a small disco bar in Berlin, the young and impressionable teenagers were gathering, for the usual weekend bash, dancing the night away. As in most European cities, this is how the younger generation met and socialised. In the bar, a man sat sipping a small beer, selling small tablets of drugs, which would enable the revellers not only to dance, but to drive them to levels of energy, that are impossible under normal circumstances. Instead of being forced to dance and rest, and to have the exhaustion of late night partying take its toll. They would now be able to dance with the enthusiasm of Chaka's warriors, all night long. The nameless ordinary girl of about nineteen had taken her recreational relief from inhibition, earlier in the evening. By two in the morning, she was as high as a kite, and unable to stand still. She dripped sweat as she danced, on the crowded boards of the disco dance floor. The place was packed like the proverbial sardine can. A heaving mass of bodies, popping to the ear splitting beat of the electric music, played at a decibel level, that would have a workplace closed down for safety reasons. The whole crush bounced, and gyrated to the base line thump, and it was hot.

No amount of extraction, or air conditioning equipment, had a hope of dealing with the heat generated by so many bodies. Sweat streamed down their backs and faces. Tee shirts were transparent in the soaking wet conditions. The humidity had risen to the point of saturation. Condensation on the small windows and relatively cooler places ran down the glass and walls like rain. Still the temperature rose. With the glimpses of near naked flesh, exposed by the wet clothing, the excitement rose even higher. Still the dancehall became hotter. On the dance floor, the centre of the room, it was like the middle of a compost heap. The biological generation of heat was rising, and the body heat had nowhere to go. Some of the party goers began to faint and drop out. They could take no more. To replace the water and energy, they drank copious amounts of sugary drinks. Cola being the favourite, it was sold at inflated prices. The one commodity that would normally accompany such a festival of freedom, was conspicuous in its absence. No alcohol for these people - It killed off the effects of the ecstasy. Much better to drink water, gallons of it.

The tiny girl felt none of the warning signs. The heat and sweat were shrugged off as a mere irritant, and the obsession to dance drove her to new heights of euphoric writhing. There was very little hint or warning. Like a racing car that had been driven flat out, and suddenly breaks down. One minute there is control of a thoroughbred, fit, powerful, and intricate piece of machinery, being driven to the limits of engineering ability. A few seconds later there is a loud, expensive sounding noise, and the engine self destructs under the strain. All she felt was an overwhelming sense that something was wrong. She felt very ill indeed for a second or so. Then came the loss of physical control of her limbs, a loud whistling, and tinnitus like noise afflicted her ears. She could no longer hear the music, as loud as it was. Then she felt her head beginning to swell. She thought it was going to burst open. Her eyes widened as her eye balls began to protrude from her skull, under the pressure in her head. Her vision clouded over with a red mist, as the blood pressure attempted to force its way through her veins. She knew no more. The effects of the hyperthermic lack of heat loss, cooked her blood in their very veins. It clotted as it flowed from a life giving liquid, to a gelatinous lump of viscous slime. She had fainted on her feet, and was dead before she hit the floor.

Chapter Five

Weatherfield had come to a decision. The recreational, and designer qualities of ecstasy, were held by those who did not know what they were talking about, to be non addictive. As there was a possibility, that his customers would not form a habit, he arranged for the use of heroin to cut the drug with, just to be sure. With the hundreds of miles of open ground on the Sino-Russian border, he was sure it would be a relatively easy task. He planned to bring in opium from the notorious 'Golden Triangle', for processing in his plant, right in the heart of Berlin. The great thing about having opened up such legitimate connections, in the chemical industries, was that his illegal importation of raw opium, from the far East, could be disguised amongst his legitimate trade. Anyway it didn't matter much. If there were any minor problems with border guards, he could pay them. The bribes would amount to a minor pittance, in comparison with the value of the cargo. If there were any officials that didn't see things his way, the occasional reminder with a Kalashnikov AK47, would keep them in line. There were always hill tribesmen, who could be blamed for the act. For that matter, he thought, there was enough latent resentment for the old Soviet regime, that he could probably pay them to do the job for him anyway.

After a few short weeks of operation, vast quantities of heroin, ecstasy, and amphetamine sulphate, were being manufactured and distributed throughout Europe. There was no stopping it. Denis Weatherfield had now become a very wealthy man indeed. Infact more money had been made in one month, than he had turned over in the previous five years. The only market that he had not penetrated, was that of Britain. It was important that he make an impression on that market, because he could distribute into a market that realised between twenty and twenty-five pounds per tablet of ecstasy. He was manufacturing at a cost of less than ten pence. With such street values available to him, the wholesale prices would be that much better. The only problem that he could see, was that on his home turf, he did not want to be seen to be involved in any shady deals. There is no organised crime syndicate to appease as such, but his first rule, of never taking advantage of those who could take revenge, still applied. He was sure that some of his entourage, knew someone who was prepared to take a risk, to courier his stuff across the border. There was that slime ball, who gave him the inside line on the German contract for one. He was not to be trusted with any information. A specimen with the loyalty of that character, would be a loose cannon, given the wrong information to spread about.

Weatherfields' instincts were right as usual. His uncanny knack of intuitively knowing, exactly how to judge a situation, bordered on a sixth sense. He was a positive genius, at guessing the capabilities of his men. He knew it, and trusted his natural instincts enough, to follow them through. It just might be that this man knew someone, who could fulfil his plans. At home base, he made contact with his man, by arranging a further game of golf, with the chairman, who he had recommended his man to in the first place. On the fifth tee, as an aside, he enquired about the man he had recommended, and if he had turned out to the good. Things had turned out better than even he had thought. Not only was his plant a trusted member of the board, but not in the least suspected. His nine handicap partner was complaining about losing the contract to Weatherfield's bid. He sportingly offered congratulations, for the brilliant accuracy of the pitched bid. Being the cynic that he was, Weatherfield paid for lunch.

The contempt that he felt for his spineless industrial spy, bordered on disgust. He loathed the lack of fidelity of the man, who he saw as a transparent tart. A prostitute to the highest bidder.

The conversation began with reminiscences over the past. The leaning began over the next half hour. The reminders of favours given, were never successfully countered, by past information given. No matter what the value of the service, it was never enough. Weatherfield had no intention of letting this one off the hook. The dirt on him was big and deep. The pedestal upon which he had been hoisted high, was shown to be precarious enough to fall off. It was a long dark view down to the bottom, and a very long way at that. After about twenty minutes or so of squeezing, the pips began to squeak to the right tune. There was an acquaintance. They had done some sailing together, when they were at the same college. They had also done some drinking, and a little blow together occasionally. He thought that through the grapevine, his friend, Heslop-Brown, was up to something, but no-one knew quite what. The verified facts were that he had teamed up with three others, and that they had been selling blow around town, in mentionable quantities. People were flocking to buy it, and there seemed to be enough to go round. Rumour had it, that he was working for someone else, because there was no flash car to show, for all the stuff he had been moving around. The truth he thought, was that the money was being saved for something, maybe a house or something similar. Finally that Heslop-Brown was known to work for himself, and was not a ten percent man.

Weatherfield bought a train ticket, and booked in to one of the better hotels in town. Not one of the big upfront places, but a family owned business. He wanted a quiet visit to the city, without attracting any attention at all. With this in mind, he bought a cheap suit , and left the Armani at home with the Gucci shoes and Rolex watch. Four members of his 'sales team' went with him. They stayed at the same hotel, and held a meeting in one of the rooms every morning. They had coffee sent up to the room for the meeting. To all outsiders, it looked like a sales promotion team that had arrived in town to do some canvassing. In fact a map was marked out, with every pub, club, snooker hall, night spot, and cafe in town. All four went out every morning to visit as many as possible, to find their man. It didn't take long. Missing out the smarter places, that looked good for shepherds pie and half of bitter, they narrowed the search to the back street public houses. On the first day, they found someone who knew him. He was used as a guide, and paid a few pounds to take them

to him. On day two they met Heslop-Brown in a small cafe, in the centre of town. He looked very cagey indeed, and was about to bolt for the back door. Assurances were made, and half believed. Mr. Weatherfield wanted to see him about a business proposition. If he liked he had been recommended by a mutual friend, and was being head hunted for a job. When an invitation was offered to dinner later, rather than a baseball bat offered to go now, Brown reluctantly agreed to go.

During the afternoon he met his three partners, who all agreed that if he didn't turn up, he would not find out what it was all about. If he did there was nothing to lose. They agreed to be there to back him up, and that the shotgun, from the boat locker, would be left in the back of the van, which would be parked outside, in case of trouble. The meeting began in a very frosty atmosphere. For the first time in his short career as a dealer in illegal substances, Heslop-Brown began to appreciate the dangers of the business. The people that he was going to have to deal with, were just as unpredictable, and dangerous as the goods themselves. That was without thinking about being caught.

The room was filled with Weatherfield and his gorillas. The desk between them might as well have been a brick wall. The atmosphere rendered the central heating redundant. Suddenly the cavalier, devil may care Heslop-Brown, felt very vulnerable. The flat, ice cold stares of the 'business associates', just failed to blink quite enough, not to be reptilian. Brown was worried. He wasn't even sure that the shotgun insurance, in the van outside, would be good enough, or quick enough, to save him if it came to it. He was convinced that these pro's were tooled up, and prepared to use their guns with pleasure. Weatherfield in his accurate guess, of how to best start off, melted the hard look on his face. He smiled and rose to his full height. Holding out his hand, he offered a warm handshake. This had the desired and pre-planned effect, of disarming Brown, and confusing him at the same time. He didn't know how to react to this mortal enemy, turning out to be his best friend. After introducing himself, Weatherfield warmed into a honeyed charm, that would have talked the birds down from the trees. The atmosphere changed to the point where the only thing that was not melting, was the ice in the mini-bar, which was thrown open with a flourish, for inspection and selection. They talked for a few minutes, exchanging trivia about the weather, and the price of bread pudding. A pregnant pause gave the in for raising the subject of the meeting.

'Do you know who I am laddie?'

'No'

'Well it may come as a bit of a surprise to you, to know that I know exactly who you are'.

'Oh.'

'You are dealing in cannabis, and have moved several kilos over the past four weeks. Before that you were a nobody, and you haven't spent the money yet. Those are the facts, now let me guess the rest'.

Andrew Heslop-Brown stood with his mouth agape. He was completely mown down by the fact that this perfect stranger knew so much about his activities. If he knew, then who knows who else knows? He thought that they had all been so careful.

''You either fell madly in love, and want to buy the house on the hill, without the inconvenience of a mortgage', continued Weatherfield,' This past month being a one off deal. That would make you cool, calculating, sensible, and level headed. Or you fancy your chances on muscling in on big time supplying. You bought and sold that blow, to finance a bigger deal. That would make you reckless, crazy, stupid, and in possession of a death wish, from the governor of the manor. On the other hand, you could have a hell bent desire, to get your three square in a cell for the rest of your life. Me, I'm no romantic. I will go for the second guess. Would you care to fill in on the details? Oh and please don't mess me about, I don't have a sense of humour today'.

One thing that got right up Andrew Brown's nose, was macho men, trying to be tough guys. He simply asked what Weatherfield wanted, and ignored the bluff with the contempt that it deserved, or at least at a level he thought he could get away with.

'You didn't go to this much trouble to find me, so that we could swop this crap. So why don't you just tell me what you want? Let's begin with how you know me.'

Weatherfield looked as though he had been slapped in the face. Nobody had spoken to him like that since he had been a boy. The man before him had no idea of just how close he was to having his ribs kicked in, just to teach him a little respect. He smiled with a half grin, but just for once, the eyes agreed with the mouth, as they smiled in unison.

'I like the cut of your jib laddie, you've got front I'll give you that. My contact was right. He is someone on my staff, who went to college with you. Who he is, is not important. You can rest assured that your operations have only been looked at by me: Also that you came highly recommended as a sailor.

I have a business proposition to put to you, which will go no further than this room. The rewards to yourself and your crew, will make you wealthy by most standards. I must warn you however, that the consequences of a leak of information, outside of the people in this room, will result in your death, and the deaths of your associates. No chances will be taken, that any security leaks will occur. Do I make myself clear? Should you wish to hear the proposition, it will be assumed that you agree with it, in principal anyway. If you feel that you do not have the stomach for it, say so now, and you can walk from this meeting. Before you answer I will say this, it is my guess that this past month, you have worked to finance a little importing yourself. If this is the case, then I can tell you that your decision should be made easier. What I have in mind, is carriage of some property, at the same time as you import your own goods. That is as far as I am prepared to describe things as they stand at the moment. If you agree, I will explain in greater detail after dinner. If not you may leave now.'

'Where's the menu?'

'Good man. I knew that I could depend on you. The fact is Andrew, that as much as I would hate to interfere with your

own operation, I wonder about the certainty of your planning. Do you have a contact on The Continent?'
'Well I was going to...'
'I thought so. You see, you will lay yourself wide open to exposure before you even start. And what about being ripped off? I don't suppose that you have any covering plans, should you get screwed by your suppliers over there. You do not have the man power to start with. No. It would be far better, and more profitable, I might add, to join forces with me completely. Keep the money that you have, and tell me what you hope to do, and when.'

Weatherfield had a very pleasant surprise, when he discovered that there was a thirty-six foot yacht, converted for trafficking, and ready to go.
'Today is Wednesday, and I feel that going this week would be rushing things. Give me a week, he thought out loud. Let us say Friday week; that will be the ninth. I will finalise details by then, and get word to you by hand. Be at your usual lunchtime location, every day please, and for now, get rid of all the blow that you have. Stay squeaky clean for the next week. There should be nothing that attracts attention to you in any way. From now on, this will be done, in a professional way.

By next week I should have the main dealers lined up. There should be an offshore delivery with a bit of luck. I figure it better to be caught with money than gear. There will be no more risk than simply bringing in some illegal money.'
It all seemed simple, too simple.

Within a week a courier came down with direct instructions. There was a fishing boat out of Whitby, which would meet the yacht, at a pre-arranged mark. It will be at a well charted wreck, well off the coast. The drugs were to be collected in Holland, and would be handed over on collection of the money. They would then return to Plymouth with the cash, hand it over, take their cut, and walk away. The four of them moved onto the boat, living their day to day lives in the marina, and preparing for the day of departure. If nothing else, Heslop-Brown was a good skipper. Safety gear was checked and double checked. Flares; chemical lights, life jackets, and emergency water supplies were layed on. They went out into the channel every day, to learn the ropes, and to become accustomed to the deck space, especially in the dark. He split the four of them up, into two watches, and made sure everything was working Bristol fashion. One of the most impressive things that these young men had been bullied into, was to work as a team. Brown knew that the attitude of drinking mates had no place on a boat in the middle of the North Sea. He had begun the first day with a lecture. It was not his style really, and made all the more impression because of that fact. He reminded them that if he wanted sail changes, he wanted them now, not in a minute. He pointed out that if it came to it, their lives could depend upon doing as they were told, when they were told.

On the tide of the next Friday, having had all passports stamped, and the boat cleared, they moved out into the channel. He had kept up radio contact with local fisherman that he knew, on channel ten, but now switched the V.H.F. receiver to scan. This would monitor the working channel 67, and the emergency and official channel 16. Passing the coastguard lookout at Rame Head, he picked up the handset, selected channel 16, and depressed the key.

'Brixham Coastguard, Brixham Coastguard, Anna-lee radio check please over.'

Within a couple of seconds the reply came back from the Coastguard station at Brixham

'Anna-Lee, Anna-Lee, Brixham Coastguard, receiving out.'

All the formalities over, he set the genoa and mainsail on a course through the busiest shipping motorway in the world.

'Left at Dover, and straight on for Amsterdam', he joked with his mates.

Chapter Six

As professional as Heslop-Brown's approach to his sailing was, so the captain of the coaster Germaine's was sloppy. Captain Walker was sloppy by any yardstick. Brown's yacht was prepared for sea with the attention to detail, safety, and planning, of a military operation. Captain Walker's vessel on the other hand, was a rust bucket, which was so poorly maintained, that it bordered on the accusation of un-seaworthiness. The ship had not had a lick of paint in years. There was some indication, that at one time, the hull may have been a universal red, with a cream upper deck. It was now a uniform off hue, with lavatory stains of rust, running down the sides. In the fleet, his ship was nicknamed ‘The National Trust’, after the Cockney rhyming slang. The vessel was a reflection of the state of mind of her captain. He was as depressed as his ship looked. His crew were infected with the same kind of apathy. The lack of enthusiasm on board, was due as much to the fact, that nobody could do right for doing wrong, as it was to her Lord and Masters' drinking.

Walker considered himself a victim of the system. He sat brooding on his future, or more accurately, regretting his past, over his half empty drink. He sat alone, as was his usual habit. He had the unenviable capacity to sit in a crowded room, and feel totally alone. He had manned his post, at the dockside bar, for four hours. He wasn't even sure which bar it was. For that matter he had to think for a while, to conclude with any certainty, which dockside he was on. He had chugged across the seven seas, for more years than he cared to remember. There had been thirty years of service in the merchant fleet, man and boy. In that time he had worked for the same shipping line. It had itself changed hands twice in that time, and the vessels, under their different owners had changed little. In 1985 the company changed. That was the most unusual event that he had seen. Within the structure of the firm, the personnel had remained exactly the same. The same people owned it, and the same crews ran it. The only difference was that the ensign, on the stern of each ship had changed. He had sailed under the red ensign, Dutch, Greek, and various other flags. The change to Panama, was of course a registration under a flag of convenience. It heralded the most painful, and drastic changes, to the way he was ordered to run his ship.

Of late things had become much worse. The crews that he was sent, by head office, without any consent, or consultation with himself, were terrible. What made it worse was the fact, that as captain of the ship, his authority had been undermined. As far as he was concerned, accountancy motivated pen pushers, who did not have a clue about the difference, between the blunt and sharp end of a ship, were telling him what to do. He treated them with utter contempt. He recalled with a wry chuckle, a fax that arrived for his immediate attention, some months ago. The document stretched to five sides. It demanded responses to previous instructions, and threatened dire consequences, if not responded to immediately. He recalled that he did respond, straight away. The fax rolled off the printer in the London office, with a one word answer and a signature;

'No. Walker.'

The animosity prevailed, and as a result, he always got the grubby end of the market. The very worst in crews were sent to him as a matter of course. It was a kind of unwritten warning on the firm, that if one was threatened with a posting to The National Trust, it was the end of the line, and the officer concerned, knew his job was on a short piece of string. Captain Walker, no-one could remember his given name, would only tolerate being spoken to, if the address was prefixed with his title. Woe betide anyone, who was foolish enough to make the mistake of dropping his title, in favour of a mister. Sir was just about tolerable, but the only thing that would more or less guarantee, the prevention of a diatribe of abuse, was the captain's title. After all it was just about the only thing he had left. It was normal after serving the company for a good number of years as a faithful skipper, to be promoted to a land based job, when ready for it. Captain Walker had been overlooked for promotion twice. He would have left to join another shipping line, but he suspected there was a conspiracy of rumours about him. They were all unjustified in his eyes, but he suspected that they thought that he drank too much.

In truth he was reputed to be a tiresome whinge. His evil temper had lost the ship, every good officer and crew that had made the error of signing on her list. The only reason that he was tolerated on the staff was that he managed to keep the unruly, low paid misfits on his ship, working the vessel from port to port. His long suffering wife had tired of it years before. She had put up with the stingy amounts of money, which had been deposited in the bank every month. She had worked herself to feed and clothe the two boys. As they grew a little older, to all intents without a father, she began to become disheartened. When it reached the stage of dreading the coming leave, because of the violence and mental abuse, she divorced him. He of course blamed her. It was all her fault, because, she did not keep the children well disciplined whilst he was away. If she would only run the home properly, and manage her money whilst he was absent everything would be rosy in the garden. He absolutely failed to see the need for such unnecessary items as shoes and clothes. One day a wag described him as fair. After all, he treated his wife, his children and his dog with equal consideration.

Having decided that it was Newcastle, he deduced that this must be the fifth. If that was the case, then had been in port too long. The very last thing that he wanted was the London office sending someone up to snoop and criticise. It wasn't as if they came to look over the ship, they didn't even know which was his ship. He doubted that they would ever find it in the dark. The only way they would know The Germaine, was if they could read her name across the stern. All they would want to do is ask foolish questions about the paperwork. It was after all, bad enough since the fax machine was invented, without the added indignity of having some snotty from the office, telling him what to do. No, he would load his cargo as soon as possible, and leave port on the next available tide. Another reason for his moving so quickly was that he didn't want to lose any crew to the enticements of residency in The British Isles. He would not be the first skipper to lose foreign crew as illegal immigrants, and if they were caught, the paperwork was endless. He much preferred to keep them as busy as possible. They were working double watches at the moment, and rest periods were confined to ship, and the bar at the end of the dock. Captain Walker was holding station in that bar, to make sure that nobody was able to jump ship.

The members of the crew were indeed a motley lot, in both senses of the word. They were both desperate for the most part, and made up of altogether different races, colours, and creeds. Many had signed on at their port of origin, as a last bid to escape either wives, irate fathers, or the local police. They would go anywhere on the globe, except for the place they left in the first instance. They were certainly a nest of magpies. If it was not nailed down, it tended to be redistributed, and Captain Walker would not have been surprised if there was the odd murderous one amongst them. He did not ask too many personal questions, about their private reasons for signing on The Germaine.

The resentful air on board was a physical presence. The only thing that all of the men had in common, was that they passionately hated their captain. With that at the surface, they only did the bare minimum of work that they could get away with, to satisfy a man, who could find cause for complaint, no matter what. If the ship was loaded according to the book, and the cargo was laid in the holds, in exact accordance with the manual, it would still be wrong. There was always something, so they did not bother with anything. The holds were filled, and the last part of the cargo was ready to be craned on board. It was a 100 tonne load, of 4x4 timbers, which was to be taken around the coast to Falmouth. Why the hell they wanted to ship a load of timber from Keilda to Cornwall, he hadn't a clue.

Perhaps they wanted to fence off the forest around Dartmoor. Frankly it was none of his business, so he would just take it around the coast, and dump it as requested. The assurance came that the wood was going on board within the next five minutes. It would be loaded, and strapped down on the fo'c'sle deck, within two hours. Walker visibly relaxed. His shoulders fell, his brow un-creased slightly, and he retired back to the bar for the duration. The wood began to arrive on deck, and the crew began to batten it down. They heaved up the nylon straps, along the ratchet grips, until they were tight. The trouble was that they did not check that the beams were settled down level in the first place.

Captain Walker's return to the ship was the unannounced signal that they were on their way. The worse for wear, but not so bad that he could not stand, all traces of bottles, and tins were removed from the bridge. At about ten minutes before the top of the tide, the pilot arrived. He guided the coaster out of the river, and the jurisdiction of the harbour. With a shake of the head, he let the boat go on its way.

It is a strange thing, the law at sea. If the pilot wanted to declare the captain unfit to take the helm, he would have to report it to the captain himself. If he thought the ship unfit for sea, again it is the captain who is lord and master of his vessel. Even if it were sinking, nobody can legally board a ship, to effect a rescue, unless the captain of the ship declares himself in distress. So it was that this ships officer, as drunk as a lord, sailed into the North Sea, without a thought of the responsibility, should there be an accident.

As with most of his voyages, this one was going none too well. There was no weather to speak of, but already some of the cargo in the forward hold had moved a little. The skipper went mental. He not only lectured for an hour and a half, on the stupidity of his officers, and the incompetence of the lack lustre crew. He also allocated blame, to everyone on board that he could think of. Quite what the loading of the cargo had to do with the cook, no-one was sure. They were in no doubt however, that he was being blamed. After a short and cursory inspection below decks, a team were sent into the hold, to tighten things down. A Heath-Robinson affair, of sealing wax, and string having been set up, to stop the cargo moving around. They would all be relieved to arrive at Falmouth, and offload the wood from the deck. At least the centre of gravity would be lowered a little. They all hoped it would be all right. It would only be until tomorrow anyway.

The day had started badly, and it went downhill from there. Hurricane Stanley was unusual in several ways, two of which were, firstly that it had a male name. The only one previous to that being David some years ago. Secondly it was one of the winds of the season, which tailed out all the way across the Atlantic. For the most part the hurricane force winds of the Eastern Seaboard of The United States, turn inland over the coast of Florida, There they die out over the land. If that doesn't happen, they turn North, and wear themselves out fairly quickly, up the Eastern Coastline. Eventually they petre out to a strong gale. Very occasionally a wind turns back into the sea, and can almost cross the ocean completely, without much loss of its phenomenal force.

Hurricane Stanley was an example of a wind such as this. The blow had originated in The Caribbean, as a reaction to tropical heat causing the air to rise rapidly. As the heated air rose up to the stratosphere, so the cooler air at sea level was sucked in. The hot air, cooling in the altitude, plunged back down to the sea. Soon the movement of air became so rapid, that it uprooted trees, in its unspoilt rush to prevent a vacuum in the atmosphere. In The Americas, these demonstrations of nature's power they call Hurricane, in the Pacific, Typhoon. For the Englishman, whose umbrella is turned inside out, in autumn, by a mere zephyr of a force five, they are beyond the imagination. These ear screaming blasts, shriek fear into the heart of the bravest souls. Storm force ten or eleven is terrible. Force twelve on the Beaufort scale, is a force that will instantly shred the sturdy canvass sails of a ship o' the line to shreds of rags.

Stanley had moved out of the Florida Keys, and headed harmlessly out towards the North Atlantic. He ripped around the globe, with nothing to stop the vast flow of air. The seas were piled up on top of one another, until massive waves broke across the vast expanse of water. By the time it had reached Ascension Island, the wind was still a good force ten. It continued on its path. It funnelled up the English Channel, at severe gale force nine.

Germaine was making fifteen knots, and was about twenty miles off Start Point, when the swell began to increase rapidly. Captain Walker for all his faults, had been long enough at sea, to know when a big blow was imminent. The waves had risen from a gentle two feet, to a four foot sea, which was visibly giving a pitch to the weight of the boat. Within the hour, the wind was whistling around the bridge, with enough anger to cause comment. In an hour and a half, the sea was boiling, with a nasty yaw added to the motion. The sloppy load inevitably shifted, as she pitched on a heavy wave. With a complaining groan, the ropes below parted, and The Germaine did not right herself. She was left with a 15 degree list to starboard.

The timbers on the fo'c'sle deck, settled with a clatter. The moment they moved, they took up that much less space. Perhaps it was only half a timber in width, maybe less. The resulting slack in the restraining straps, gave 100 tonnes of timber enough momentum, to drive straight through the ropes, as though they were not restrained at all. With that peculiar rising complaint, the woodwork groaned over the side. It seemed to pause at the gunwale, as it climbed over the two feet of freeboard. It was as if to cock a snook at escaping from Captain Walkers' Jonah boat. Finally and inevitably, it went over the side, celebrating its freedom with a resounding splash, and floating up in a jumbled chaos.

It was at that precise moment, that Captain Walker, master of all that he surveyed, knew that his new title was going to be mister, about thirty seconds before the board of enquiry closed. He looked at the bottle of scotch on the instrument panel, by the wheel. He picked it up, opened the bridge doorway to leeward, and heaved it overboard. That was the last drink that he ever handled.

Chapter Seven

As with most investigative police work, detection is more a process of elimination than verification. The formation of a hypothesis, and the building of facts around it, is the complete reverse of what actually happens. The facts are taken, and all irrelevant leads, are eliminated from the enquiry. Then all that remains are the unanswered questions. If all goes well, the facts, and the questions without answers, point in the general direction of a suspect, or a number of suspects. There was not much hope of holding out for a single fingerprint match. In the first place, the material had evidently floated inshore. There was nothing concrete at the moment, to suggest that the original handlers, were of British origin, except for the fact that the money was in Stirling. It had also been handled by The Wilsons. As simple as the elimination of their prints seemed, it was a fact that they may have smudged anything that was there in the first place. There was the salt water too. The packages could have been in the sea for days, if not weeks. The courts would require at least sixteen matching points, to accept a comparison of one fingerprint with another. They would accept two prints, with a ten point comparison, if each print was from a different hand. The possibility of lifting such evidence, from the material available, was very slight indeed. The location of the find was not much help either. Anywhere else, and a date of losing, and finding, would give a possible calculation, with tide and time, of the point of origin, or there abouts. Some years ago, a fisherman was lost, not far offshore, in The Sound. Oceanographers were able to calculate, where the body would turn up, three months later. In twelve weeks and a day, the remains turned up, within a few metres of the predicted place.

From the place that they were found, the money bags could have come from anywhere, even inland. The rivers Plym, Lyner, or The Tamar itself, could have been the source of the parcels. They could have floated into The Sound from The Channel, and in the end there were hundreds of square miles of water, both fresh and salt, that could have been the place where the money was lost. There were no real clues there. Of the money, it was established that it was real money. The serial numbers were of notes that were currently in circulation. They were all used, and there were no consecutive wads. There was nothing that could give an indication of the area that it came from, let alone an individual bank. All that was left, was a bundle of black plastic bin liners. There was hope here, because it was known that manufacturers often supplied direct. In this case, it was direct to Nurdin & Peacock. The most widely spread wholesale cash and carry chain in the country. The bags could have been bought, in any corner shop, or canteen in the country. That left the tape.

This was the break that they had hoped for. Forensics had established several special features about the green tape that the bags were bound up with. One of the scientists, in the laboratory, looked at the green tape, and was curious as to why ordinary two inch parcel tape had not been used. Commandeering a roll from the post room, a short experiment soon revealed the reason. Basically it did not stick. A short phone call to Sellotape, who manufacture such tape, was met with an enthusiastic offer of help, and an invitation to bring a sample to the factory. The technical director, took one glance at this pale green tape, and identified it immediately, as plating mask tape. He also said that he could offer several pieces of information, which the police may find of value.

In the first instance, perhaps by coincidence, they had come to the right place. The tape that was offered for inspection, manufactured in that 12m.m. size, is exclusively manufactured by themselves. It is called Plating Mask Tape, which is of course identified by its green colour. Thirdly it is exclusive, in being chroma discharge treated, which is necessary, in order to be able to adhere to plastics. Further it is chemically inert, to prevent any reaction with the work being masked. It is made with a high adhesive mass. That is to say, there is a lot of glue, all over the adhesive surface of the tape, in order to ensure a good bond. A sixth point - It is easily removable. A roll of the green tape, was produced from his pocket. He stuck up a black plastic bin liner with it. The tape was ripped off, and there was no trace of glue on the bag. The next point, they were told, may be of particular interest to The Police. It is used exclusively, in the manufacture of printed circuit boards. Its specific use, is to mask off the circuits, on printed circuit boards, in order for the electrodes to be gold plated. The ninth piece of information is an economic one. It is ten times the price of ordinary parcel tape. Lastly, and probably most importantly, this tape is not available from any retail source. The only way that this product, could appear in this usage, is via the electronic printed circuit board industry.

'In short sir' he said, 'your man probably scrounged or more likely stole, a roll or two of this stuff from work'.

This was all very well, but there were hundreds of users, all over the country. Back at the station they had to decide what to do, and the best way to go about it. The team came to the deduction, from the facts, that there were two possibilities. Tied together, they could lead to a suspect. These were that their man worked in the electronics industry, and secondly, that of late he was at sea, or at least not at work.. The only other question that could be asked, was whether anyone was missing any rolls of Plating Mask Tape. It was very doubtful however, that two rolls of consumables would be missed by a manufacturing company, which used the stuff all the time on the production line. They decided to ask the question anyway.

The next problem that they had was how to reach all the people in the industry, without attracting attention to The Wilson family. The periodical magazine for the trade is a monthly glossy, which takes advertising, up to three weeks prior to going to press. This meant up to four weeks before their information was targeted, and that was far too long. In the end, with nothing to lose, they decided on the Crimewatch UK television show. With a bit of mystery, as to why they wanted to know, they asked for anyone in the industry, who uses the tape, and has responsibility for staff records, to give them a call. There was an overwhelming response, of five calls. The whole team sank into a state of depression. At five minutes to midnight, a managing director, who had been out at a charity dinner, had returned home to be told by his family, that the request had been on the telly. He picked up the phone, and called the number. His Plymouth factory was not all that large, and handled specialist, rather than volume work. The name he gave to the police was very interesting indeed. He had left three weeks ago, without so much as a period of notice, and had not even called back for his holiday pay. This had struck him as odd at the time, because Lee Carpenter was always short of money. For him to fail to call in for his holiday pay was something of a mystery. The name was put through the computer, to Criminal Records Office. The C.R.O. sent back a report of petty crime, that went back years, and it included the usual theft violence, and car crime. Such offences are hardly aptly named. It is difficult to see the funny side of joy riding. There were a couple of petty drug offences too, but nothing big, and no hard drugs were in evidence. Still they decided to bring him in for questioning, if only to eliminate him from their enquiries.

CID had all four faces in mind for something, for some time: Andrew Heslop-Brown, the social misfit and his three stooges, Carpenter, Pengelly, and Fisher. It was obvious that they were up to something, though it was generally thought to be both petty, and disorganised. To be able to link the four of them in, with what appeared to be a haul from something so big that it had to be organised, was a surprise. So much so, that it was probable, if not obvious, that they were connected. That these men, the wanna-be captain of crime and his three must-get-beers, could be connected with serious criminals, was almost a joke. The nagging connection, between Carpenter, and the tape, was going to be investigated to the limit.

What was needed, to project this from being a list, into a theoretical story, was a second, or even a third piece of information, which gave a pointer, in the same direction as the first. In view of the fact that the money was found in the sea, they began to make checks with the marine connection. There were no known friends in the sailing fraternity. Those who knew the characters in question, did so at a distance. They were known, but only as people who were available, to be used as replacement crews in a race.

The rock solid break came from FreeMed Charter. It was not the charter of the Jenneau that was half expected. The lucky bit was the tale of the father, giving the money. One telephone call, to a disappointed, desperate, and defeated Mr. Heslop-Brown senior, confirmed that he had done no such thing. He had no idea where his son was, or where he had obtained the money, for the charter of a yacht. Frankly he didn't care anymore. Where his son had gone wrong, he did not know. The time had passed when he blamed himself, now there was only resignation, and the constant waiting for the police to call. He always hoped it would be prison. He didn't think his heart would stand up to the ‘I think you had better sit down sir’, beginning of a visit. He dreaded the day.

The money in small doses, was believed to be a diversion. It was widely thought that there was a financier involved. The established fact was that Brown had lied to get the boat. The other fact was that he had acquired the money from somewhere. The clever money thought that he had been grub-staked.

Chapter Eight

It would seem rational to most people, that a yacht, worth about £80,000, being crewed by four young men, and sailing into Amsterdam, would attract attention. Such a simple concept went right over the head of Heslop-Brown, and he just sailed into port, in broad daylight. He hired a berth for a few days, and paid for it in cash upfront. In the same light, it was unusual for Weatherfield to make big mistakes either. Because there was so much money at stake, he rashly decided, to make the delivery personally. In an attempt to confuse any would be watchers, the boat was berthed at the marina at Den Helder.

The situation was perfect really. In the first place, he did not fancy his chances, against all the shipping in the port of Amsterdam proper. There is a hundred miles or so of coast within the harbour, and several very large docks. The shipping moving in and out of there, could accidentally dismast her at least. For that matter, they could turn her into matchwood, without feeling the bump. Den Helder is right on the point of the harbour, and the open sea. The marina is protected by Texel Island. The last island south, in the archipelago of land, protecting the main harbours from the rigours of The North Sea.

Having paid for a berth for a week in advance, they locked up The Anna Lee, and headed for the town. They travelled separately, and each bought a return ticket to Amsterdam, from the booking office of the local railway station. The regular service soon put them into Amsterdam Central Station. They met up in the square, and walked out onto Prins Hendrickkade, and east to the notorious Zeedijk canals. The area is only two hundred yards from the station, where drug addicts share the streets, and often their needles, with the prostitutes. Having walked around the compulsory circuit of the tourist track, they headed back towards Prins Hendrickkade.

They met Weatherfield at the previously arranged Shrierstoren, or Weeping Tower. This was the place where sailors were said to say their goodbyes to their womenfolk. It was built in 1487, and a tablet marks the point, where Hendrick, or Henry Hudson, set sail on The Half Moon, on 4th April 1609. This was the voyage that took him to what is now New York. The river, bears his name to this day. Today the tower is a reception, and exhibition centre. There is also a book shop, which they browsed around, trying to look like tourists. The Dutch policeman, in the polo shirt, check jacket, blue slacks, and brown brogues, looked even more like a tourist. The two officers with him, looked like fellow travelling companions. The classic man and wife team, with a gooseberry companion, carrying a camera.

The 'man and wife', stood outside the weeping tower, by Henry Hudson's plaque, posing for a photo. Ten yards away, Weatherfield, Brown, and his team, walked out of the shop doorway into the street. The tourist pointed his camera, and told his friends to hold the pose. Weatherfield, being very wary indeed of people wielding cameras, turned round to face the cameraman for a second. He was about to cross the street, to confront him, when he realised that it was just a tourist. The lens was pointing at his friends a few yards away. He dismissed the incident as unimportant.

The Nikon F4 35m.m., has a programmable exposure setting, and computerised focus. The motor drive will shoot six frames a second. The clever bit was that the 24m.m. wide angle lens, even though it was pointed at the plaque on the wall, put Weatherfield, Heslop-Brown, Carpenter, Pengelly, and Fisher, in sharp focus, on the right hand side of the pictures. They didn't even know that they were the stars in a new version of Candid Camera. It was not as if any of them had done anything wrong. It was just a matter of policy, to keep an eye on unusual boat arrivals, around the port of Amsterdam. When they walked straight into the red light district, trying to look like holidaymakers, and then met another man, in such an obviously pre-arranged fashion, it was decided to take some mug shots, just for the book. They were followed around the corner, back into Prins Hindickkade, and Weatherfield was noted to enter the Scandic Crown Victoria Hotel, opposite the station. This is one of the better hotels in the city. It is also one of the older establishments. It has that plush air of distinguished class, which is only attainable, with the maturity of the years. The types of clientele that are looked after so well there, are not the sort that are normally to be found in The Zeedijk area, to the rear. The specific arrangements for the handover, had been made earlier, in the bookshop.

The return train to Den Helder, left at 4.30p.m.. The four went into The Scandic Crown lobby at four fifteen. They were shown up to Weatherfield's suite at 4.17. By twenty minutes past four, they were on their way down in the lift, with a large sports bag. There was even a squash racquet zipped into the racquet pouch. The more important contents, were a plastic bag, within which were sealed, thirty kilos of ecstasy tablets. At a weight of around 0.6 of a gram each, that is £10,200,000 worth at twenty pounds per tablet, street value. Sold wholesale to dealers, they would make half that, or just less. The actual price made was £150,000 per kilo, or a cool 4.5 million.

At 4.25p.m., they were walking across the square, and into the central station. The train was in, and they were on it with a minute to spare. The delivery had gone like clockwork. They had not been followed as far as they could tell. They were wrong in that respect. The police officers tailing them were dedicated experts and they had a good idea that they would return to the boat, so they did not crowd in too much. There was a four man team of followers. One was in the lobby of the hotel, who alerted the rest of the team, as soon as the four of them left. He then moved station to the end of the street, in case of a split up. It had been decided if there was a split, to follow the bag man. He after all, would be the one in possession. There was another on the railway station platform, who followed them onto the train, and sat in the next compartment to the one that they occupied. There was also an officer at the front, and another at the back of the train. If they decided to play games, and move about the compartments, they were covered. The officer on the ground could still see the station square, and if any of them jumped the train, just as it began to move off, he could call for back up on his radio, and wait for the target to emerge from the station square again. As was predicted, the bag man moved to Den Helden station. They were watched as they boarded the Sundance 36, Anna Lee, and a binocular watch was kept from a nearby house.

On board Anna Lee the sports bag was opened up, and the squash racquet gashed overboard. Heslop-Brown went into action, being careful at the same time, not to become effected by the highly potent cargo. He didn't mind getting out of his head at parties, but he was not going to do it now. Negotiating the waters around the port of Amsterdam, and The North Sea, whilst out of your head, is not recommended. From the tool locker, near the battery compartment, on the port stern, he donned a dust mask, of the type used by construction, and demolition workers. He also put goggles on, and a pair of medical gloves. Amphetamines can dissolve into the sweat on the surface of the skin, and permeate into the bodily system. Whilst handling such vast amounts of the stuff, it is vital to wear protective gear. Lifting the forward accommodation bunk lid, he exposed his new extra water tank. The Stilsons, once again, separated the filler from the outer skin of the collapsible tank. The whole lot, including the inner false bag, were removed. The employment of a large funnel, and the removal of the corner of the delivery bag, ensured the smooth pouring of all the tablets, like a liquid, into the false tank. With a little shaking around, they settled in nicely. The inner false liner was eased into the filler aperture, and the filler screwed back into place, for the second, and last time. The use of cotton waste, to prevent the flats from being scratched, made the final job almost impeccable. The last thing was to fill the inner bag, with 25 litres of water, and it sloshed around convincingly. It was as though there was nothing untoward hidden in there in the first place. They were set to leave, and did so, just after midnight.

The team investigating the whereabouts of Lee Carpenter, and Andrew Heslop-Brown, had come to the conclusion, that they, along with possibly the two others, had left the country, in the chartered yacht Anna Lee. There was no evidence to suggest that they had told the truth about their destination, or the reason for the trip. They felt that the circumstances were suspicious enough to alert Interpol. An approach was made to the Detective Chief Inspector, in charge of the investigation. The view was endorsed, and permission granted to contact the international force. Within a few hours, with Interpol making the more obvious enquiries on the behalf of the British Police, the information began to gel into a story. The Marseilles Police had no idea. There were several Jenneau marques in the port. Of the Sundance 36, there were two. None were called The Anna Lee. The force in Amsterdam, simply asked for a fax number to send the photographs to, and if they wanted an immediate arrest.

The decision as to whether to haul in the five eels in the trap, or to wait and see what else slid into the net, was a tricky one. They were fairly certain, that the five could be arrested at any time, and that there was enough proof to convict no matter what happened. The boat could easily be followed, and arrested on the high seas if necessary. The temptation to see what else would crawl out from under was too entising to pass up on. A general request to continue with surveillance only, was broadcast to all the forces involved. When the pictures arrived, they were as sharp as a David Bailey photo-call. There were five beautiful, crystal clear mug shots, of all five men. At last things were looking up - The chase was on, and Customs and Excise, and The Coastguard Service were brought into the picture, with a request to find the boat.

'You have got to be joking'.

The simple rejection was a slap in the face. The coastguard on the other end of the line began to explain.

'Firstly there is the fact that the radar scan covers the shipping lanes and not the whole North Sea. Secondly there are hundreds of vessels out there, from all destinations. They are calling to all the shipping ports, from Northern Russia, through Scandinavia, into Holland, Belgium, France, and then there is the Scottish, and English traffic. That is a rough guide to the international shipping on The North Sea. That traffic passes day and night. Also there are the fishing fleets, domestic traffic, and private boats to consider. Add to that the fact that such a small boat would probably not show up on the screen, unless it carried a radar reflector, and you will begin to see the picture. If they don't want to be found, they would be bloody daft to leave a radar reflector at the top of the mast, wouldn't they?

Now if they are carrying an E.P.I.R.B., in the safety equipment, and if it accidentally sets off, then we will find them in fifteen minutes. Then again if they are daft enough to pick up the V.H.F. handset, and transmit on channel 16, the signal can be triangulated in half a second. Unfortunately they will have to give the name of the boat over the air, at the same time. In short, you have two chances. A snowball in Hell, and Naff all sir, sorry.'

As they were back at square one, they had no choice but to wait until the boat showed up somewhere, and the details were transmitted to all ports authorities, with the priority of finding her emphasised.

It appeared as though the yacht Anna Lee had disappeared for a while. When the options, which were open to the crew were considered, finding them seemed even more hopeless. They even included slipping into a little French port for a week or so, to indulge on the wine and good food. The list of places to go was almost endless. It was increasingly obvious, that they were engaged on an impossible task, for the moment. This game of chess was being played out, and at the moment, it was their move. Heslop-Brown had headed Anna Lee, on a basic bearing of 270 degrees. This would take him more or less directly East of Amsterdam, and directly for the coast of Britain. The Decca Satellite navigation system, gave him a position on the planet to within 100 metres. On the more or less Eastern heading that he had chosen, he approached the English coastline.

The wreck chosen, was a none too well used position. Fishermen had given it a hammering over the years, and there was not a sprat left, worth baiting a hook for.

Consulting the chart room, he selected chart number 1408. This covered The North Sea, from Harwich, to Terschelling, and

Cromer to Rotterdam. The Wreck was marked at Latitude 52o 30'N Longitude 002o 32'E.

As part of Weatherfield's ever widening business empire and because he owned, or bought out a lot of companies outright, he had ended up in various trades. Most of these oddments, he had no intent upon in the first place. As an example of this, he had bought a construction company in the Northeast, which was a parent in itself. Before it had been taken over by the bigger fish, it had owned some other smaller firms. There was a small pottery, and craft shop, which had more to do with the managing director's wife than construction. There were various other acquisitions, one of which was the trawler Lympne. She was a Scollaper originally, and was registered at Newlyn, in Cornwall. She had fished out of Whitby for a number of years now, landing Hake, and Cod when she could find any. When the company was stripped, the boat was kept on as a P.R. exercise, as much as anything.

Local people were worried that jobs would be lost in the take-over. The man who had previously been at the helm, had a philanthropic concern for the area, and its people. As the fishing boat seemed the more at risk, from a company that was primarily concerned with construction, the fishermen were guaranteed their jobs in writing. The publicity at the time, was high profile, and made the front line of the local rag. The local radio, and newspapers, were so full of interviews, and stories, of the good fate of The Lympne, that there was no room for the story of the joinery shop being closed. There was a loss of six skilled carpenters, and twenty-five office and ancillary staff. Instructions had been taken by hand from Heslop-Brown, to the skipper of The Lympne. The message was simple.

Admiralty Chart 1408 Lat 52o 30'N Long 002o 32'E: 00.30 hrs 10-11 June V.H.F. Channel 10 - NO repeat NO communications Channel 16 24 hours previous - Skipper Anna Lee. They were not going to risk being triangulated at the meet.

The sail from Amsterdam was very gentle. They had allowed two days, for a day trip, and were reaching across a nice force four, with the mainsail, and foresail jib.. The Genoa was packed away, and awaited the run down the coast to The

Channel. From there they planned a simple cruise down The South coast, and back to Plymouth with the money from the exchange. There was so much time to spare, that they relaxed a little on board. A nice hot meal was produced from the freezer, via the microwave oven. They indulged themselves, with a long relaxing smoke, of some very nice Dutch cigars, which they had found time to shop for in Den Halden. As dusk approached, at around 20.30 hours, they moved into the horizon of the meeting point. The wreck, being fifteen miles offshore, is below the horizon from the coast, and is far enough away from the main shipping lanes, to be a backwater. At around 23.30, navigation lights could be seen on the far horizon, about ten miles off. They sailed towards the wreck, and marked off the course from the Decca.

There are four satellites in particular, which are floating around the globe. At any one time, as one clips over the horizon, another appears above it, on the opposite side of the sky. The Decca sends a radio beacon, up to the satellite, and the satellite notes the exact position of the source of the signal. It then transmits back to the machine, telling it exactly where it is. This information is displayed in figures on the LCD display. That information is upgraded, every fifteen minutes. To plot a course, to a given point, is not as difficult as it was in the old days. Captains Bligh, and Cook, 'shot' the sun, with a sextant. Those days were indeed long gone. True to form however, Heslop-Brown had one, knew how to use it, and had one on board. The fact is that a sextant may be archaic, but it cannot breakdown. There were no other ships on the horizon, and as V.H.F. works in line of sight, it was probably safe to make radio contact. The two vessels were on a converging course, about three miles apart, and the mark was a mile from the yacht.

'Lympne, Lympne: Anna Lee, Anna Lee over.' The squelch on the ether hissed for a second or two, whilst he listened on the channel. Channel ten is used more or less exclusively, as a working channel for the fishing fleet. There was little likelihood that anyone was going to be tuned in to that channel, at that time of the night.

'Anna Lee, Lympne, I see you ahead. Pull alongside; over.'

‘O.K. see you in fifteen minutes, out.’

Unlike the world of Hollywood, nobody uses the stupid and superfluous sign off 'over and out'. It actually means nothing, and makes no sense. How can you pass transmission over to the other radio operator, and end your own reception at the same time? The other radio operator will have nothing to transmit to, after all, you told him that you are no longer listening. Attending to the vagaries of wind and tide, Brown started the engine. After five minutes of warming up, he engaged the forward gears, and turned up to wind a little. Having taken the strain off the sails, he ordered that both be lowered, and loosely reefed up out of the way. He fixed the boom, and now they were ready. With two minutes to spare, they came alongside Lympne, and warped up to her, on her lee side. As the yacht had a deeper keel, she was the more likely to drift down the tide, so Brown pulled her alongside on the lee side of the wind. Such masterful, and respectful seamanship, gave no hint that Mr. Pengelly was below, just below the hatch.

In his hands was the Remington 870, pump action shotgun. The same weapon used by the S.A.S. The magazine was loaded with eight cartridges of special S.G. At nine balls to the cartridge, pointed in the general direction of a person, it is a very effective weapon. All that would be left is a head and a pair of legs. There was also a ninth round, in the breach. The precaution was a mere insurance against the skipper of the other vessel, who may get ideas of becoming greedy.

In truth the captain of the fishing vessel, had no real idea what was in the packages that he had been asked to deliver. He had a good idea that it might be drugs, of course, but he didn't want to know. His job was to deliver the parcels to The Anna Lee, collect a parcel, and return home. He was told that someone would be waiting for him, with an envelope, which contained five thousand. The rest he didn't care about. They were both working for the same man, so there was little probability that one would try to double cross the other. There was also the fact that anyone who had any sense, was too frightened of the consequences, to consider doing the dirty on

Weatherfield. The switch was completed in ten minutes or so. The warps were cast off, and Lympne was headed for home.

Heslop-Brown, who hated wallowing around, dead in the water, gunned the engine, and turned around to 180°, a directly Southern bearing. As the boat moved on, they unreefed the sails and continued in a comfortable motion. Having found the wind, he disengaged the Morse drive, and cut the noisy engine. After the smell of the exhaust had dispersed, they were once again in the peaceful realm of the summer ocean. Heading for the quiet cove of Gorran Haven, in Cornwall, they went to meet the man who would make them rich. Two days of plain sailing, would make it as easy as shelling peas.

Chapter Nine

From the wreck off the Norfolk coast, where the rendezvous had gone so very well, Anna Lee was bound for the South coast of Cornwall. For a moment or so, Andrew Brown considered the possibility of going the long way, all around the coast of Scotland. He would go down the West coast, the Bristol Channel, and around Land's End, The Lizzard, and in to Gorran Haven. The route had its advantages. For one thing, he had never done The British Coast before, and calling in to all those unnecessary harbours, and Marinas on the way, would make it look even more like a holiday trip. On the other hand, he was carrying a large amount of money, which belonged to one of the worst animals he had ever come across. He sometimes thought that he was a bit over enthusiastic with his ideas. Sometimes he was even a touch obsessive, especially he thought, when he could not get his own way. He tended to brow beat a little, until he won. He had never seen the likes of Weatherfield before. The man was utterly ruthless. People followed him, not because they though that he was a good leader to follow, but because they didn't fancy being knee-capped if they didn't. Even by his standards, the man was a nutter. It was probably going to be safer, as well as wiser, not to keep him waiting. The Straits of Dover were going to be a problem.

A small sailing vessel, negotiating the busiest shipping motorway in the world, was not a venture to be taken lightly. With bulk carriers, container vessels, and oil tankers thundering their way through, thirty-six feet of fibreglass, did not seem much at all. It was a bit like taking the dog for a walk, down the M25 at rush hour. Not to be recommended to the faint hearted. They would not, under any circumstances, be undertaking the passage in the dark. The wind was Northerly at the present, and was to veer to the East, dropping from a force five to a three. It was then expected to back around to a Southerly 5 again, as the low pressure area passed over The North Sea, towards the West. Once passed Dover, they would expect a Southerly influence, from The Atlantic, up The Channel. Providing that they obeyed all the navigation rules, and kept to their allocated lanes, then they would be safe. The Straits of Dover, is the only bit of sea that is so busy, that it has been necessary to split it up into directional shipping lanes, to enable traffic to navigate safely.

As dawn approached, Anna Lee was about fifteen miles off Southend. With the favourable wind, they would go through the straits without having to tack more than once. That was very pleasing, as the criss-cross, hazard, across the shipping lanes, was nobody's idea of a fun time. Andrew was glad that he had stuck with the rules. Without the benefit of the chart of the straits, and the knowledge of how to read them, they would have been mowed down, like a Hedgehog on a highway. As it was they were skirted by a bulk carrier, which went past like a floating office block. The steel walls rising twice the height of a house out of the water. By the end of the afternoon, they were starting to relax a little. The area running in to The Solent, and a little closer to shore, is more ideal water for sailing yachts of the Jenneau's character. There arc no tankers to have a row with at any rate.

Having made such good time, they decided that they would call into Poole in Dorset, for the night. They would be able to go ashore at least, if only one at a time. They had been a few days at sea, and already there was friction at the untidiness, and the smell of sweaty socks, was becoming a little gamy. If they stayed overnight, each could have a run ashore, to put his wash through the launderette, and perhaps have a slap up meal, in the cafe of the marina, whilst they were there.. Skipper Brown insisted that they only go one at a time. They were not going to leave the money unguarded. All went smoothly, and they settled down in the accommodation, for and aft, for a good night's sleep.

There is an extremely large market, on the coast of the South and Southwest of England, in stolen chandlery. The amount of V.H.F radios, logs, satnavs, and buoys warps, bric-a-brac, and fishing gear, that goes missing is enormous. The men had launched into the harbour in a pram dinghy, with the oars wrapped in rag, around the rowlocks. They could slip from boat to boat, and check each for their security. The more modern boats are secured with deadlocks on the hatchway, and would require breakage to enter. The noise would amplify in the water, like the sounding board of a musical instrument: Too loud for opportunist thieves like this. The older vessels, especially the wooden ones, are sometimes simply padlocked. All it takes is a screwdriver, or a jemmy under the hasp, and they are in. The radio is the first to go, then the rest of the gear. It all disappears into car boot sales, and is never traced again. As the dinghy bumped alongside, they all awoke at the same instant. It was the fear motivated reaction, which lifted them from deep sleep, to wide awake, in an instant. The two thieves could not believe their luck, that the yacht was unlocked. As the door opened, the Remington was brought up to bear.

It may be that one of the reasons why pump action shotguns are so popular, with police forces around the world, is that they often do not need to be fired. The metallic racking action, and the noise of the cartridge, being cranked into the chamber, is enough to put the fear of God into anyone. In the dead of night, in a quiet harbour, on the coast of Englands' green and pleasant land, it prompted a reaction which was as dramatic, as it was fast. The two of them went backwards over the stern. One hit the dinghy, but with only one foot. It overturned, and hit him in the back, as he went in the drink. The other took the more direct route, and just hit the water. They scrambled the little boat over, and clambered in, bailing out with their hands, and splashing away from the gun, or the devil, as fast as they could scramble.

The moment of danger and anger had passed, and Messrs. Heslop-Brown Carpenter, Pengelly, and Fisher, looked at each other in the moonlight on deck, and burst out laughing. It was probably a combination of a lot of things, that caused this hysterical, and uncontrolled, primeval laughter. The joy of the victor that had defeated the foe. For sure that was part of it. It was surely a release of a lot of strain, and tension that had built up over the last couple of weeks. The risks that they were taking, were far more enormous than any of them had considered. Were it not for their arrogance, and the devil-may-care attitude, that is common to youth in general, and them in particular, they would probably not be doing this trip. If they had half a brain each, they would probably be dangerous. There was also the laughter at the irony of their situation. If the nickel and dime, light fingered thieves, had half realised what was on board, there is no knowing what they might do.

The realisation that this was exactly the type of trick that they were up to only a month ago, made it even more funny. It was as though this moment, was the agent which gelled them as a team. As much as they had worked together in the past, and these were friends of long standing. This seemingly small incident, joined them as a unit, that almost anticipated the needs of the other three. They began to do things for the benefit of the boat, rather than as an instruction which needed following. As a result, not so many orders and instructions were needed, and tasks were willingly anticipated. That too released a lot of pressure and tension between them. They knew in their hearts now, as well as their heads, that nothing could stop them. All they had to do now, was stick together, do or die, and all would work out. With the attempted piracy of their loot, they untied from the moorings, for and aft, and quietly slipped out to sea, in the very early hours of the morning. The false dawn, was just giving an indication, of the coming of the morrow, and all was well. The hop from Poole, down the coast, was but a day's gentle sail. They almost called in for lunch, but thought better of it. Taking a needed night break was one thing, tempting providence, on the other hand, was plainly silly. In the morning light, with the sun rising behind them, they set the foresail, and main, to cruise down the coast, in no immediate hurry. The mast of The Anna Lee was kept below the horizon, all the way down the coast, so that if they were being watched, they could not be seen from land.

Incredible though it may seem, there is no way of tracking a boat down The Channel, except for physically following it. A yacht will not show up on radar, nor is there any radar surveillance of traffic down the coast. The overstretched Coastguard service, are hard pressed to carry out their existing duties. With the budget that they have to work in, they cannot afford to chase hunches and shadows. By the end of the day, the tide had changed, and the sunset lit up the Western sky, with mauves, greens, gold, and violet. The whole evening sky, was a backdrop, which could not be rivalled by even the greatest of artists. In the early night, the whole sea was washed with the gold of the rising moon.. As it climbed higher in the sky, it appeared to become smaller, and changed to that ghostly silver of romantic beauty, so fondly spoken of by the poets.

There is something so overpoweringly wonderful, about sailing a yacht, in a gentle sea, by moonlight. It goes far beyond all the well-worn clichés, which have been used to describe it. The feeling of spiritual fulfilment is almost overwhelming: The complete peace and serenity of the silver sea; The hint of incandescence, as the tiny, myriad creatures of the deep, fluoresce in the foaming wake, the black depths, making the soul so insignificantly small, in the vastness of sea and sky, the countless stars, with no street lights, and towns to drown their beauty. Andrew Heslop-Brown, was taking his watch on the helm. He loved this gentle type of sailing, and promised himself a brand new Jenneau Sundance 36, when he was paid.

His face hit the stainless steel rim of the wheel, with a sickening crunch. One of the last things he heard, was the bone in his nose crunching, as the flesh that surrounded it, spread across his cheeks. He heard and felt the sharp agonies in his right arm, as it had slipped between the spokes, when he was catapulted into the helm. It had snapped at the same time as the socket of his arm popped from the shoulder. It felt as though he had been kicked very hard, and then a hot knife was slid in between the joints. The two bones of his forearm glistened clearly, with the wet blackness of his own blood, in the moonlight.

A large plank of wood 4x4x5 meters long had slipped between the keel, and the rudder in the water. The instant drag, was like a massive sea anchor, and the boat had shuddered to a dead stop almost instantly. It might as well have hit a brick wall. The aluminium mast snapped and fell forward, billowing with the ghostly shrouds of its sails, which wrapped themselves in a funereal drape, over the Anna Lee. The rudder could not take the strain, and parted from the hull, with a sickening rip. The ear splitting screech, made his teeth ache, as though the spirits of a thousand teachers from hell, had walked the chalk down the board, to attract the attention of their errant pupils. The resulting one foot square hole, filled up the yacht with water, at an incredible speed. There was nothing that he could do. There was no time to release the liferaft, and anyway, he wasn't sure that there was anyone left uninjured, and above decks. The men in the accommodation, had no chance. As an instinctive cry for help, he plucked the handset from its hook, and depressed the key to transmit. The auto search, would automatically tune to the emergency channel 16.

'Mayday, Mayday, Mayday. Mayday, Mayday, Mayday. This is the yacht Anna Lee, 5 miles south of Eddystone'. Those were the last words that he managed, before the beautiful sleek lines of design, and elegance, sat up, and went down.

He never did realise, that the very first water to enter the bilges, at the stern, soaked the batteries in sea water, and rendered them useless. The cry for help, was never sent, let alone received on the lonely nightime ether. He didn't know why he was choking in fumes either. The salt in the sea water, reacted with the battery acid, to give off chlorine gas. He was coughing his lungs up, like a first World Warfare victim, before he had even hit the ice cold water. With the shock of the broken bones, and the cold of the sea, he lasted no more than ten minutes. His brain dulled to the point where he had forgotten how to swim, and what land was for, and then gave up. The other three died, trying to find out which way was up, inside the plunging hulk. As the water rose, in the ever decreasing space, their ears began to bleed with the increasing pressure. In the blackness of the coffin like saloon, the salt water burned their lungs as they tried to breathe. Then they just passed out and drowned. All that was left, as evidence of the existence of The

Anna Lee, were a few clothes, dhan buoys, and a few black plastic bin liners floating on the surface.

Chapter Ten

After a week, Weatherfield had become a very angry man. The merchandise had definitely arrived on the mainland. The whole market was flooded with ecstasy, all over the country. After a meeting with his contacts, and an assurance that the money had changed hands, he was now convinced that Andrew Brown, and his mates, had decided to be too greedy with his money. It was not just the money either. It could not be seen, that anyone was able to rob him, and get away with it. They must be found, and the money retrieved. Summary justice would be metered out with a vengeance that will set an example. It cannot be allowed, to let it be seen, that Weatherfield could be mugged. The sales team were dispatched to Plymouth, and the search was on. It would not be hard to find them, if they came ashore. The grapevine of information that he had set up over the years, meant that not much went down, without him knowing about it. Rumour, gossip, and bravado, are the easiest forms of communication to follow. The skill is in sorting out the wheat from the chaff. Infact all the gossip that came his way, was noted, and if the same tit-bit came his way twice, then he took it that there was something in it. He was a great believer that all lies are founded in truth, and even the wildest claim, can be boiled down to a verifiable fact, somewhere along the line. The first rumour that he heard, was that the boat had left the country, and that it had not been seen in port, anywhere along the coast.

The fact was that they were supposed to turn up at Gorran Haven, and that they had not arrived. There was a faith in Weatherfield's mind, that Brown was not as stupid as that. In the first place, he could be rich and free, and to choose to be even more rich, and to hide for the rest of his life, was not clever - especially as he could always do it all again. They would be killing the goose that laid the golden eggs. Secondly there was the yacht. They could not steal £100,000 pounds worth of boat, and hope to get away with that either. The charter company would be looking for it all over the world. His instinct told him that something had gone wrong. They had not been arrested, that was for sure. If they had, there would be news, and press reports, all over the media. There had not been a squeak. There might be a chance that someone else had got wind of the operation, and had decided to rob them of their spoils. In which case, the boat would be playing cat and mouse with the pursuers, until contact could be made with him. There had been no contact yet, and it was now a week, so that saving grace, was rapidly running out of credibility.

In all the usual hangouts, they drew a blank. Nobody had seen any of the four sailors. A check at work, had revealed that Lee had still not turned up for his severance pay. If they had done a runner, that fact would be surprising, but there was not a hint. It might have been expected, that a contact would at least be made with his family, or girlfriends, but there was nothing. They had all but given up the search, and decided to go out for a drink in one of the night spots in Union Street. After all, what they did not find out at ten o'clock at night, they were not going to find out at one in the morning. It was by pure chance, that they decided to move away from the noisy dance area, and into a quiet side bar, to discuss tactics. As they were sat in an alcove table, they could overhear the loud conversation, of the animated young woman, in the next booth.

As they listened, they could not believe their luck. This girl was describing, in loud and graphic detail, that she had seen a man, picking up parcels from the beach, at Devil's Point, right across the road from her flat, loaded them into his car, and then drove off with them. She told of her exiting interview with the police, and how, sleuth like, she had taken the car number, and given it to them. She went on to explain how the nice police woman, had taken the trouble to explain to her, that it was rubbish that had been thrown overboard in The Sound, that the police had traced the ship, and were going to prosecute. Wasn't she a wonderful, environmentally conscious person? The sales team, didn't believe a word of it, and having overheard the general area of the address, they left for the car.

The A-Z street map told them that Devil's point, and Durnford Street, was only just around the corner. There was only one end of the road, where Devil's Point could be clearly seen, and only one house with a window that looked out in the right direction.. They sat in the car, and waited for her to come home. In about half an hour, they were rewarded with the arrival of a taxi, and the self same girl, paying off the driver. She crossed the road, and walked into the Victorian house. The hall light went on, and she made her way upstairs to her flat. They confirmed their observations, when the light in the room overlooking the car park went on. The silhouette of the same figure closed the curtains. They sat in the car for a while, until they were sure that there was nobody else about, and then they got out, opened up the boot, and took out their tools.

Sarah Birch accepted, the same as most people do, that the day to day ordinariness of her life, was quite comfortable. The humdrum lack of excitement, was balanced with the comforting predictability, of what was about to happen next. The old joke about the fact that it must be Wednesday, because it's Shepherd's Pie, expresses that admirable comfort in life, and the prediction of the sureness of tomorrow. Having her usual moment of peace, and her dawn coffee at the widow, interceded by that man picking up drugs or something from the beach, merited comment. It was up there, on the same level as spotting a film star, or a famous politician, in Woolworth. It was the highlight of her week, and held her as the centre of attention, in her circle of friends, for days. She had spoken of it at work, at the cafe at lunchtime, whilst out shopping, and in the night club, on Friday night, where she joined her friends for a late night dance. It was not that she was a gossip, but it was very exciting. She opened her big mouth once too often. Weatherfield's Henchmen, were good at their jobs. It was not that hurting, and bullying people was the clincher in the job description. It was the power of the infliction of terror, and the awesome tyranny that made it so attractive. Before approaching the door, they made sure that they had their equipment to hand. It didn't look much, just some hand tools in a canvas bag. It was there intended use that was so petrifying. In a shoulder holster, one carried a gun.

As a result of the Hungerford massacre, when one man went berserk, in that quiet country town, some of the laws of gun ownership in Great Britain were changed. The ownership of any automatic assault rifle, by anyone, no matter who they are, is now banned. The weapon is considered an unnecessary, and overly dangerous one, to have in the hands of a privateer. What is not widely appreciated, probably due to the emotive publicity, which was quite understandably involved at the time, was what actually happened there. The assault rifle, was not the weapon, which was used by Ryan, to inflict the most damage. The Italian manufactured, Baretta 92F, is a most formidable piece of armoury. In an urban environment, where the target is likely to be within a range of 35 metres, or less, it is a most popular weapon. In street, there is likely to be a brick wall to hide behind, at no more than 30 metres. A weapon with any higher range, is not needed. Indoors, a rifle is almost impossible to handle. It cannot be turned, and aimed on a stairway, or in a doorway. Much better to have a handgun. An automatic sub-machine gun, like an Uzi, or The S.A.S. favourite, Hackler & Koch, has its advantages of fire power, but cannot be concealed under a coat so well.

The semi-automatic Baretta, hides neatly under the arm. A good bespoke tailor, can hide it almost completely. Weighing only about four pounds, with a fifteen round magazine, which will fit into a jacket pocket comfortably. It can be drawn, loaded, cocked and fired, in four to five seconds. The clip can be unloaded, the weapon made safe, and holstered just as quickly. The magazine clip is ejected by a simple button, on the side of the stock, left of the trigger guard. It is loaded by simply sliding it home, into the handle of the pistol. The cocking mechanism, slides back with the left hand, and a lever on the left, above the trigger, can be flicked with the thumb. This projects the first round into the chamber. When fired, the cartridge case ejects, and the cocking mechanism, automatically reloads the next fourteen rounds, which can be fired off in less than six seconds. When fired, the explosion is a dull heavy crack, and the inexperienced would find a tendency for the weapon to rise up, and to the right. With practice, a nice centre body pattern can be achieved. The brainless thug on the other end of this piece of engineering ingenuity, was carefully selective of his ammunition. After all, he made it up himself. It is illegal in this country, to buy live ammunition. It is not illegal however, to buy cartridges, powder, percussion caps, and bullets separately, and make them up at home. The weapon was bought in a pub, and the cartridges, were loaded with 124 grain, steel jacketed 9m.m. slugs. In this instance, the intent of the weapon, as explained, was to inflict fear, not pain, it would not need to be fired. The enormity of its very presence, would be enough for a simple shop girl.

The disbelieving peak of mental rejection, the infliction of mind numbing pain. The point where the victim would say anything, anything at all, except lies, because the truth is the only sanity that is left, would be achieved by other means. There would be no preliminary questions, to put her on her guard. There would be no amateurish slapping about, or the threat of sexual abuse. No ripping of clothes. There would be nothing, not at first.

The three handed team, approached the Durnford Street flat, at about 2.30a.m. They knew that she was still up, and that her flat door was at the top of the first flight of stairs, straight in front. They walked up the three granite steps, from the street, into the town house. The front door was not locked. It served as a service door to the other, as it happened, unoccupied flats, and bedsits, in the house.

Two fourteen pound sledge hammers were produced, and with one crouching, and the other standing, they swung the hammers, in a sideways motion, like a discus thrower. They stuck, and penetrated the hinges simultaneously. Much better to remove the two lightly screwed hinges, than bother with the locks, bolts, and inevitable security chain. The door simply fell flat on the floor, in the passage, and Miss Birch came running to see what was going on, with a shocked look of disbelief on her face. It was not as shocked and disbelieving as a few moments later. The hammer men discarded their redundant tools, and each took a four pound lump hammer, from the canvas bag. Earlier in the day, for a few pence each, they had bought six, six inch copper boat nails, from the chandlery. Each nail being square cut, parallel, and about 1/4 of an inch thick. They had slipped a two inch diameter mudguard washer over the point, up to the half inch cut end, to prevent any slippage. The third man grabbed her by the throat, with one hand, and cupped his other hand in her crotch. He bodily lifted the slight, six stone girl down the passage. Not a word had been said. She did not know what this was all about, or why it was happening. She thought she was about to be robbed, and raped. She was wrong on both counts.

With the third man holding the body weight, each arm was stretched out to the top of the door frame. Two nails were carefully placed in the wrist, just above the junction of the forearm bones, and quickly driven home, with the lump hammers. Her thumbs reflexed across the palms of her hands, as the nails smashed the nerves controlling them. Her legs were spread apart, and four nails, one into each of the joints of her knees, and one through each ankle, were smashed into the door frame. Then they let her go, watching her, crucified on her own living room doorway. There had not been a single scream. She was just pinned there, in a state of absolute terror, and shock. They watched her heave her body upwards, to relieve the pressure on her diaphram, and suck in a large breath to scream out. As her mouth opened, a rag was stuffed into it. Now they very quietly, deliberately, and calmly, asked her a question.

'Where is the man who found the packages on the beach?'

She shook her head. The rag was removed, and she blurted that she did not know. She was menacingly reminded, almost in a patronising whisper, that they knew she had seen a man collect their property. Furthermore, that she had told the police of the matter, and that she knew the registration number of the car. Would she be kind enough to let them know, what the car registration number was? She told them that it was on a piece of paper, on her notepad, by the phone. They found it, where she said it was. She said that she did not know anything else about him, and that she had never seen him before, or since. They believed her implicitly. The Baretta came out, and in a smooth action, was loaded, cocked, and three rounds emptied into her head, in less than four seconds.In another thirty, they were in the car, calmly driving towards Millbay Road, and the busy night club area.

Chapter Eleven

All that glitters, so we are told, is not gold, and what had started out as a simple drug smuggling lead, had grown into a nightmare. It appeared to be a simple matter of waiting for the charter yacht to appear on the Southwest Coast, and arresting the crew. That was to be followed up with the arrest of Weatherfield. The catching of the big fish, along with the smaller ones, had the sweet aroma of promotion to it. Over the last seven days, it had gone terribly sour.

The wreckage off the Devon Coast, was beyond doubt that of The Anna Lee. There had been no sign of a liferaft, or any bodies. All four were posted missing at sea, presumed dead. Any drugs that were on board, were now 50 metres down in The Channel. Then there was this Wilson character, who suddenly turns up, with bags full of money, and the forensic scientists, had very quickly come up with nothing. Then there was this green sticky tape, Plating Mask Tape, but putting the tape in Carpenter's hand, from the factory to the boat, would need a confession. That would be difficult with the possibility that he was feeding crabs at the bottom of the sea. The fate of the one and only witness, had been the most sickening murder that had been seen on the force. There was little doubt, or at least there was a high probability, that Weatherfield was responsible for the murder. He had personally ordered the death of the woman, which was no doubt carried out by his employed thugs. All that was required was to connect it all together.

There was now some considerable concern for the Wilson Family. If they had found Sarah Birch so easily, then there was every possibility that they would find the Wilson's in the same way. It was accepted that Miss Birch had told them everything that she knew, before she died, and that they therefore knew the registration number of the car. If there was access to the police information, via a leak, they would find out within a minute, who the owner of the car was. If not, it was still not difficult, if not actually as quick. All that was required, was a form from the post office, requesting a copy of the vehicle registration document, as a new owner. It will automatically arrive with the new owner registered, and the full name and address of the previous owner. In view of what had happened to that unfortunate young woman, in her own flat, there was grave concern, for the safety of the entire family of the finders.

It was perhaps the only advantage of being unemployed that he could think of, but Geoff Wilson was glad that he did not have to expose himself, by going to work every morning. In view of the danger to himself, and his family, he had decided to give up the money, which did after all, belong to Weatherfield, and walk away no worse off than he was before. The police would hear none of it. In the first place there was no actual evidence that the money belonged to Weatherfield in the first place. Secondly there was nothing to suggest that he would collect the money, and leave it at that. They would probably do something drastic to them all, just for the hell of it. They were not going to be allowed to get away with it either, and they were beggared if they were going to have a chance for the loot as well.

The routine enquiries ground on. As usual it was this dogged approach that gave a result. Teams of officers were making door to door enquiries, of hotels and guest houses in the city, to try to find where the murderers were. It was the arrogance of their belief that they were above the law, that gave them away. They had booked into the hotel as a group, under the name of a company from Newcastle. A quick check showed that the firm was a subsidiary of a construction company. And the Chairman of the board of directors, of the building firm, was Weatherfield. Gotcha!

They were arrested and banged up, in less than twenty minutes. A cursory search of the car, revealed baseball bats, hammers, a shotgun, and a handgun. The Baretta 92F, had recently been fired, and had not yet been cleaned. It was full of forensics. They were delighted. At last there had been a positive result. Four for the Birch murder. The press would be pleased that this lot were out of circulation. There was a direct connection with Weatherfield, and everything was beginning to tie up into a neat bundle. With the four smugglers missing, presumed dead, the only one left was Weatherfild. He was going to be difficult to catch. He not only had connections all over the world, he had the money to skip the country.

When he heard that he had lost his money, his men, and his chance to retrieve the cash, by the crew of the yacht drowning, Weatherfield did the one thing that he had not yet done. Over all the years of greed, and dishonesty, everything had been planned with meticulous accuracy. The most important factor of all to him, was not to be involved to the point where anyone else could prove anything. When he learned that his money had been picked up by a beachcomber, walking his dog, he finally went over the edge. The thing that finally did it, was the realisation, that the money was only his, as long as he held it in his hand. There was no way that he could hold and spend it, without careful laundering. For sure he had the legitimate businesses, to deal with the money, but it all took time. What really bit to the quick, was the fact that this little man, had a stupid lost property ticket, All he had to do was wait for three months, and nobody could touch him. While he waited, he was smug in the knowledge, that the cash was so bent, as to be unclaimable by anybody else. If he so much as went upwind of a police station, he would be looking at twenty years. That was the other galling thing. He was now wanted, and he could not afford to wait for the ninety days, to grab him, and take the money back.

It hadn't taken more than a phone call to find out who this Geoffrey Wilson character was, nor his address. There was only one thing for it. If he could not have his money, nobody else was going to have it either. He would get the kids first. He would watch for them, and find out where they go to school, where they go out to play, and get them. Then his wife. It would be a great pleasure to watch his face, as he watched her die. Then him. The idea of watching the man suffer, would be the greatest pleasure of all. The plan was a simple one, he would go to the school, and take them out there. In the morning, he sat in a hired van, dressed in working overalls, watching them leave for school. They were only tackers, probably eight or nine years old. So they had to attend one of the two schools for infants and juniors, local to their flat. They walked to school with their mother, and at the top of the road, turned to the right.

Weatherfield started up the van, and drove around the block. It was a country mile to drive all the way around, but he didn't want to be seen to be tailing his victims. Across the main road, and into the side streets again, it was all more or less the same. An ex-council estate, with much of the muchness dispersed by the right to buy scheme. The boring red brick, and concrete sameness, broken up with white cement paint, and Canterbury spar. The style was now very much pebble dash, and plastic windows. As the street narrowed, the school came into view, on his right. He stopped with all the other traffic, which were mostly parents, taking their children to school.

He took his tool box, a cheap blue, metal box affair, with two handles. He had half a dozen like it at home, and this one was loose change, in the local D.I.Y. store. The internal shelf had been taken out, and a few oily rags put in. The rags were there to cover up the .44 Magnum, fully loaded, in the box. It was not a necessary weapon, but it suited his ego. The massive long barrel, made it very imposing. Looking for all the world like a workman, come to either fix, or maintain something, he walked up the path, to the infants, and junior school. There was a problem. The older girl kissed her mum goodbye, and ran off, up the path, to the junior school behind. The little boy, went into the infant's school, at the front. He noted that the classroom was fairly near the front entrance to the school, and that a long corridor serviced all the classrooms. He would take the girl first, and in the confusion, run down to the infant's school. All that was needed, was to run into the corridor, open the classroom door, and shoot the boy on sight. He could then escape through the cloakroom door, into the playground at the front of the building. The rest was easy, down the path, into the van. From there he could drive down to the flat, he would kill both of them, with two shots to the head each, and then into his Jaguar, which was parked around the corner, and out of town.

Weatherfield returned to the van, and drove back around the estate to the flat. He parked up the hill, just in view of the door, but far enough away, to be inconspicuous. Mrs. Wilson walked down the road, passed Weatherfield, and the big red van. It never occurred to her to look, it was just another workman. He walked the last few yards down the hill, down the garden steps, and into her home.

Now there was simply the matter of having the patience to time his attack. The best time would be when the schools had settled down to lessons for the morning. There was always the play period of course, but the noise and confusion created by the first hit, would undoubtedly raise the alarm in the lower school, and make the second target less easily accessible. Better he reasoned to attack between lessons beginning, and break time. 9.45 seemed reasonable. There was about two hundred yards, between the rear exit of the junior school, and the connecting path to the infant's school.

There would be no need to run, a minute at most would cover the ground. The confusion after the first hit, would be such that the alarm would not have reached the bottom school. There were five minutes short, of three quarters of an hour to kill, without attracting attention to himself. In the shopping precinct on the village green, is a cafe. It would be normal for a workman to have his breakfast at this time. In his overalls, he would fit in to place. He went in, and ordered a hearty breakfast for himself. In five minutes, the cook produced a large plate of bacon, eggs, sausage, mushrooms, and all the extras, including beans, and a fried slice. The whole lot finished off with a large mug of steaming tea. The excitement of the prospect of blowing children's brains out, had made him hungry.

The great comfort to all children, is routine. The safety and comfort, of having the ability, to predict what is going to happen next, on a daily basis, is the stuff that children thrive on. If it is Tuesday, it must be swimming. So Tuesday can be looked forward to, with the certainty that it is going to be fun.

Thursdays however, are just another school day, with sums, and reading, history is nice, and geography is fun too. After meeting in the classroom, and having her attendance mark in the register, Elizabeth Wilson made her way down to the school hall, for morning assembly. She enjoyed singing hymns, and saying her morning prayers. The whole family of the school, were joined together for the start of the day.

At nine fifteen, they left the hall, in single file, and in orderly disciplined fashion, back to the classrooms, to begin the days work. The school curriculum, in accordance with the new National rules, had to begin to teach science, and scientific principles, to the children. The first lesson, was a fun time, of making practical measurements of water, by volume. They were learning the size, and look of litres. Something of a revelation to a child, for whom a jug of water was just something dad watered the geraniums with. In the infant's school, they were all in class, doing the important work of children. They were all at play, and in the process, learning the alphabet, numbers, and their relationship with the world around them.

It had been the practice at both schools, for some time, to have a classroom assistant. For the most part, this was a volunteer, who helped the teacher to organise lessons, and hold the attention of the class. In most circumstances, the volunteer helper is one of the parents, who offer their help for nothing, and rotate on a regular basis. It was not unusual, or disruptive to the children, when the classroom assistant changed. They actually liked Miss McAlister, she was great fun. The children were blissfully unaware, that she was a police officer, and that she had been on the case of the money bags, from the first day. She recalled Mr. Wilsons face so well, when she knocked on his flat door. He looked as though he had seen the ghost of his conscience past. The head teacher was blissfully unaware, that W.P.C.McAlister, had completed many courses in her time as a police officer. She was a dedicated professional, who loved her job.

In the first place, her first aid skills, were close to the qualifications of a paramedic. She was well beyond mouth to mouth, and sticky plasters. She had completed the police driving course, and much to the chagrin of some of the men, had been able to complete the pursuit part of the test, with top marks. It was this cool head under pressure, along with her magnetic personality, that had enabled her superiors to recommend her for the weapons training course. She was proficient enough to knock a neat pattern in the middle of a target, at 35 metres, which is no mean feat with a .38 revolver. Most people would miss with at least one round, and leave the others in an increasing line, ascending the target. Holding and firing hand guns is not easy.

Weatherfield had a habit whilst eating a fry up. He neatly sliced up his fried bread, into squared croutons. One by one, he dipped them into the golden runny yolk of his egg, and ate them. It was a delicate procedure, and looked somehow out of place in the manners of such an obviously big, and powerfully framed man. His habit always triggered off memories, of the previous occasions, when he had performed this operation. It was a ritual that he had used before action, all his life, and it had begun in the Marines. Having earned his green beret, one of the first assignments that he had to undertake, was a tour of Belize. The hot, humid, jungle warfare, suited him well. He went on a foray, in search of rebels, and before the exercise began, he was surprised that his fear, and apprehension had left him. In its place, was a hole in his stomach, that made him think that he hadn't eaten for a week. The only thing that would satisfy this hunger, was a bloody great fry up. In the canteen, he fiddled with his breakfast, in a ritualistic, and religious way. It was there that he developed the habit of meticulously cutting up his fried bread. In the cafe on the green, he knew that he was going to coldly massacre this family. Both his mind, and his fried bread told him so.

The clock on the wall told him that it was twenty-five minutes past the hour, and that his timing would be right in twenty. Allowing five minutes to finish his breakfast, walk over to the van, and drive up the school. He had absolutely no intention of screaming out of the car park, smoking tyres and engine, in order to satisfy the excitement of the hunt. He did not need to attract attention to himself. As the old army saying goes, softly softly catchee monkey. At about 300 metres down the road, he pulled over. The area was surrounded in grass verges, and high fences. He would not be over looked. He stepped into the back of the van, and opened the tool box.

The Hackler & Koch gleamed with its new oily smear. He loved its hard blackness, and steely coldness. Sliding back the cocking mechanism, he checked the breach, finally ensuring that there was not a round in the chamber. An accidental firing, would be a disaster. To alert the quarry early, would completely kill the mission. The clip, which was located at the bottom of the box, he unwrapped from its cotton wrap protection, with the care of a diamond merchant, revealing the awe of his wares, from their black velvet cocoon. In his final preparation, he pulled out the.44 Magnum, and slid it in the inside of his overalls. He loved that cannon. In the excitement, he almost forgot the props of his cover. He had to return to the back of the van, to collect the tool box. The walk up to the school door seemed to take forever. If he could make it without passing the office, and being quizzed by anyone, then he was sure that there would not be a major bloodbath. He never liked shooting innocent people, just legitimate targets, like the Wilson kids.

The rear door into the corridor was open, and led straight down to the classrooms. He knew that the room he wanted was the second door on the left. It was as quiet as a church, with everyone in their classes, and nobody roaming around the corridors. He felt his heartbeat begin to rise, as the build up to the kill intensified. It was a go.

He slid the tool box onto the floor, and produced the sub-machine gun. The clatter of the round, levering into the breach, echoed down the empty corridor. He froze in his tracks for a moment. The whole world seemed to slow down, as his reflexes, and his adrenaline rushed. He trotted down the side wall, and stepped quickly across the window in the classroom door. The tenth of a second glance, was enough to take in the scene. There was a roomful of kids, unaware of him outside. They were bent over their childish problems. Inside the classroom, Miss McAlister had heard the unmistakable sound of a weapon being loaded and cocked. She had spent enough time at the range to have a fine ear for such things. The rest of the class, looked up at the muffled noise outside, and decided it was someone dropping some books or something. They carried on with their work.

Taking no chances, W.P.C.McAlister went over to her bag, picked it up, and went over to the alcove at the side of the doorway. This position had three advantages. She could not be seen from the window in the door. She would have the jump on anyone coming through the doorway, and most importantly, the children would be out of her line of fire, if she had to use her revolver. She put her hand into her bag, and felt the comfortable grip on the .38. Just in case, she felt for the safety catch, slipped it off, and made sure the gun was pointed towards the books on the wall shelves. If there was an accident, at least she could be sure that only a copy of Wind in the Willows would cop it. If needed, she only had to pull the bag away from the gun, and she was ready to fire. Being the gentle minded soul that he was, it never occurred to Weatherfield, to carry the tool box. If he had knocked on the door, he could have gained entry, by simply asking to check the central heating pipes or something.

He tried the handle, then burst in through the door. The machine gun was in his hand, and he was looking for the girl, in the sea of surprised faces. The sight of the gun and the violence of the entry, was all that she needed to make a split second decision. The bag slid off her right hand, and in classical style, the revolver swung up, with the left hand steadying her right. The first round entered Weatherfield's body at chest height. It went into the lungs, smashing the rib cage, and splitting the muscles of his heart. The second soft jacketed, hollow point shell, was the twin of the first. The third round as a result of her control, letting the gun rise with the recoil, was placed in the right temple. There were three neat holes .38 in diameter in the right side of his corpse. There were three six inch diameter patches of minced meat, where the shrapnel had exited the body. For a moment in time, he thought his head was going to explode. It did, and he was dead before he hit the floor. In the afterlife perhaps, there may have been a little teenager from Berlin, who would have smiled with satisfaction.

Epilogue

The last three months had been a living purgatory to the Wilsons. The publicity surrounding the school attacks, and the death of Sarah Birch, had been a focus of the national press for a couple of weeks. All the old chestnuts had been brought out for an airing: Bringing back capital punishment being the most obvious. Some sick minded head case had a national tee-shirt campaign, with the slogan;

'Bring back Hanging, You can't bring back the Birch'. There were thousands of other sick minded head cases wearing them.

Every day was like waiting for the other boot to drop. There never was a longer ninety days spent by a family. It was not as if something had happened, which could now be allowed to pass. As the day drew nearer, the excitement rose even higher. There was a terrible desire to pick up the telephone every five minutes, to see if anyone had claimed the money. The thought that all the parties involved were dead, with extreme and violent deaths, was cold comfort to them. Little Elizabeth, along with 26 classmates, had to have professional counselling. Someone had to help them deal with the enormity of having a man shot to death, by their classroom assistant, right in front of them. They were closer together as a class now, but they would never be able to erase the horror of that day from their little minds. Elizabeth was still having nightmares. At last the day arrived, and the children were allowed a day off school, to go with their parents to the police station. It began at six in the morning, as nobody in the family could sleep through the anticipation. They skipped breakfast, in favour of coffee, and cigarettes for the adults, and milk and biscuits for the children. They could not be bothered with anything either.

They were outside the solicitor's office, at five to nine, and the beaten up Lada Riva, was parked outside with them.

Geoffrey wondered if he might keep the car as a sentimental whim. After all, it was the only thing that had served them well over the last few weeks. The dry old stick of a solicitor was waiting for them, with more coffee. Geoff wondered if there was any self help group that could help him. This guy was a caffeine addict. Mr. So and so, (he never could remember his name), had the lost property ticket, in the inevitable brown manila envelope. He had to suppress a smile, even his shoes creaked.

They followed the company Volvo, and were led up to the police station. The desk sergeant, asked if he could help them, when they walked in the door, as if he didn't know who they were, and what they wanted. Mr. So and so produced the ticket with a flourish, and placed it on the desk.

'My clients have called to collect this property, which after the ninety day expiry period, now rightfully belongs to them.'

'Just a moment sir', the officer said. He picked up the ticket, and affected long sightedness, holding the paper a distance away. He gave up, produced a pair of spectacles, which he polished first, then hung on his nose.

'Ah', he said. 'I see', he said, 'just a moment sir', he said again. He disappeared around the back of the counter for a couple of minutes. Geoffrey was hopping from foot to foot, as though he was bursting to go. He probably was. The suspense was killing him. The sergeant returned to say that they were just checking and that they would not be a moment, sir. The sergeant disappeared again. Five minutes later he came back with an announcement.

'The duty inspector would like to see you for a moment sir, would you mind stepping through. The rest of you may come too if you wish.'

'Here we go' said Mr. So and so.

They were taken to the lift. The sergeant pressed the button, and the sharp eyed solicitor began to look a bit doubtful. There is no police business that involves the public, on the fifth floor. He had been coming to this police station for ten years, and had never been to the fifth floor before. As the lift stopped, and the doors opened, it became obvious that they were entering the staff canteen. Unusually there were balloons and bunting hanging up, like it was Christmas.

P.C.Grayson, and P.C.McAlister, wearing her brand new police medal for bravery, led a mighty cheer from the whole of the police team that had been involved in the case and they popped the champagne corks as they walked out from the lift.

After the drinks and the speeches, the deputy chief constable himself came over to Elizabeth to ask if she was feeling any better. He handed over a bank account pass book for the full amount, in Geoffrey Wilson's name. The whole lot had been earning interest for him: for three months. There was now the best part of five million in the account, with all the interest. After all the thank yous and good wishes for the future, they took the book, and left. In the car park, was the little Lada, with which they did not want to part. To try to let it all sink in, they went for a stroll across the grass.

The salesman in the Mercedes dealership across the road, assured them that they would be able to have a very good deal indeed on a matching pair of his and hers SE's, and they would be able to source a suitable pair of matching number plates too. When Geoffrey placed the order, the salesman gingerly asked how this unemployed looking person, was going to pay for the cars. When he said cash, and presented the balance of his savings account, the man nearly choked.

Printed in the United Kingdom by
Lightning Source UK Ltd., Milton Keynes
137554UK00001B/415-450/P